CALL OF THE LAST SURVIVOR

AN UNOFFICIAL FORTNITE NOVEL

CALL OF THE LAST SURVIVOR

AN UNOFFICIAL FORTNITE NOVEL

KEN A. MOORE

Sky Pony Press
New York

Visit our website at www.skyponypress.com.

10 9 8 7 6 5 4 3 2 1

Library of Congress Cataloging-in-Publication Data is available on file.

Cover design by Brian Peterson
Cover artwork by William Puekker

Print ISBN: 978-1-5107-4486-8
E-book ISBN: 978-1-5107-4487-5

Printed in Canada

CHAPTER ONE

At first, nothing.

At first, only the shimmer at the farthest edge of the barrier projected by the shield device.

Mikaleh waited, her finger on the trigger of her assault rifle. It was only a matter of time. It was only ever a matter of time.

She knew that they would come.

What drew the husks to humans? It was the great, unknowable question. Unknowable perhaps as the Storm itself.

The Storm came; the monsters followed.

This was the only thing upon which everyone agreed. For many, it was all that they cared to know. It was enough.

Though it had been only a few short years since the start of the crisis, many survivors seemed only to wish to forget the days before the husks had come and the world was changed so utterly. But Mikaleh couldn't forget.

The world—the world as it had been before—was the reason why she fought. Every zombie-like husk that she sent back to oblivion with a squeeze of her trigger or the deft toss of a grenade was a tiny step toward making things right again. Every survivor she unearthed or freed could join the project of repairing the Earth and undoing what had been done.

For the moment, the surviving humans had shields to keep the husks at bay, and weapons to cut them down with when the shields did not hold. The humans also had the best parts of humanity. They had cooperation, communication, and—perhaps most importantly when you were fighting zombie hordes—construction. The ability to build massive bulwarks that could literally hold hundreds or thousands of husks at bay—at least for a while—was turning out to be one of the biggest advantages humanity had. (For all of the husks' other formidable traits, they did not seem to be particularly good at going around things placed in front of them. Circumventing ditches and funnels, and climbing over knee-high walls were also not among their strong suits. Most of the time, husks preferred to claw frantically at a wall instead of simply sidestepping it and moving on. Mikaleh had never understood precisely why this was, but she and the other survivors were not about to look a gift horse in the mouth.)

At the edge of the shield barrier, strange purple lightning flashed. Ethereal shapes seemed to materialize just at the edge of seeing. Mikaleh's finger tightened ever-so-slightly around her trigger. How many times had she stood with the other members of her squad against an oncoming horde like this? A hundred times? Two hundred? She supposed that three hundred was also not out of the question. She had stopped counting after the first ten or so. Yet the tingle of excitement that ran down her spine said this might as well have been her first. Some things never got old. And the knowledge that you were going to protect humanity, while kicking some serious husk butt in the process, was still enough to make the hairs on the back of her neck stand on end.

The raids had become a weekly occurrence now. Sometimes the husks came twice a week, or even three times. And always, her squad was ready.

The first time the husks had made an organized assault, Mikaleh and her friends had been an ordinary group of frightened survivors, huddling against the strangeness of the Storm. When unearthly monsters that looked like rotting human corpses suddenly stumbled and gibbered out of the mist, Mikaleh had scrambled madly to find her grandpa's old hunting rifle that was stashed somewhere in the basement. Her friend Janet—a strong, stocky young woman who worked construction—had hastily nailed together stray wooden pallets to reinforce the doors. And the two awkward young men named Sam and Sammy, who had lived down the street from Mikaleh—and who were so identical they might have been twins, or just brothers, or possibly cousins—had grabbed what tools and weapons they could find to help out in the fight.

And their little squad had won. Against all expectations, they had beaten back the rotting monsters and held their position. The squad had shot them down with guns until they turned back into goo. They had bashed them with hammers and mallets and pickaxes until they disintegrated into rags and splinters. They had even chopped them into little bits with samurai swords until the bits had stopped moving. It was, everyone agreed afterward, a lot easier than they'd imagined it would be. And also . . . it was sort of fun!

Many people said the secret to happiness was to do what you loved. And even in a zombie-filled apocalypse beyond understanding, Mikaleh and her friends found a way to do exactly that.

In the weeks and months that had followed, Mikaleh and her friends had built a reputation as the ablest squad of surviving humans that anybody knew. These four relished what they did. Not only did they never run from a fight, they positively ran *to* anyplace the husks were expected to show up next. Where other humans often remained paralyzed by fear in the face of an oncoming horde of husks—Mikaleh, Janet, Sam, and Sammy looked forward to dealing out destruction and mayhem on their undead enemies. As time passed, each member of their squad had seemed to naturally specialize in certain tasks that came in useful during close encounters with the husky kind. Now their actions on the battlefield seemed second nature. They worked collaboratively, but in doing so became like a single machine, honed and fine-tuned to make husks disappear as quickly as possible. They always won, and nothing surprised them.

Nothing . . . until now.

"All pitchers?"

Mikaleh risked a glance over to where Janet stood proudly atop the parapet she had constructed only moments before.

"What's that?" Mikaleh said. "What did you say?"

"I think it's *all* pitchers," Janet said. "Huh. Never seen that before."

Mikaleh looked again.

And in the strange glow emanating from the edge of the shield wall, it *did* seem that the husks zapping into existence all wore pinstripes and had all brought bags of bones to throw.

Mikaleh lowered her assault rifle for a moment. A contingent of pitchers alone was strange indeed. The husks were no master tacticians, but even they had figured out that if you only brought artillery—and artillery that threw bones, slowly, to boot—you were going to get rushed and overwhelmed pretty quickly.

"What I've never been able to figure out . . ." Janet said, leaning on a sledgehammer, "is if pitchers were baseball players back when they were alive, or if the Storm made them into baseball players. Like, maybe the Storm has a training camp somewhere that we don't know about."

"I dunno," said Mikaleh. "I'm still not convinced that husks used to be people. They could be aliens or something. Or from another dimension."

"Are you kidding?" Janet asked. "*Of course* they used to be people."

"Have you ever seen a husk that looked like anybody you recognized?" Mikaleh countered.

"No . . ." Janet said. "But there's always a first time."

At that moment, the sound of approaching footsteps made both women turn. It was Sam and Sammy, who had removed themselves from the platform where they'd been preparing to ambush the advancing husk infantry. Both Sam and Sammy were short, and wore overalls and short haircuts. They also both wore round, circular eyeglasses. Sammy carried a katana, and Sam held an automatic shotgun, but otherwise they might have been identical.

"Dudes, are you seeing this?" Sammy asked.

"Yeah," said Sam. "Are we crazy, or is it—"

"*All pitchers,*" Mikaleh and Janet said in unison.

The (possible) twins exchanged a glance.

"They've never sent all pitchers before," Sammy observed. "What do you think it means? Maybe they were getting ready to have a run at us today, but only pitchers showed up?"

"Or maybe it's some kind of holiday for the other husks?" Sam said. "Like the others have the day off? This is most unusual behavior. Definitely worth recording."

Without looking down, Sam fished a small notepad out of his pocket, and then a grease pencil. He spoke as he scribbled.

"Day #923. Husks sent all pitchers. Reasoning behind this is not yet known."

One of the only differences between Sammy and Sam was that Sam was preparing a field guide on husks. He made notes on their behavior and their psychology (such as it was), with the hope of one day authoring the definitive book about them. Sam believed that understanding the husks was the key to defeating them.

"Sam," Janet said, shaking her head. "Don't you want to wait until *after* we fight the battle to make notes?"

"This is important, and I want to record everything while it's still fresh in my mind," Sam countered defensively. "Anyway, it looks like the pitchers are really taking their time setting up."

He yawned as if to make his point.

The squad looked down from the defensive parapet where they stood to the edge of the woods where the pitchers stumbled about, looking like rumpled major leaguers who had had too much to drink (or perhaps just a very hard blow to the head). They carried satchels of bones over their shoulders from which they drew their missiles. Pitchers were not the only kind of husks who used ranged weapons, but they were some of the most distinctive. The bones they threw were big and covered with residue from the Storm that often glowed purple. Even though they were strange looking, you underestimated them at your own risk. Getting smacked hard in the face with a glowing purple bone was not something anybody forgot quickly.

"Head back to your positions, eh?" Mikaleh urged. "We'll make short work of these guys. Then I promise, Sam, you can study them all you want. Take as many notes as you like on why they showed up alone."

"Fine," Sam said. "Also, like always, remember where we are and look out for crossfire."

The defensive barriers Janet had constructed were designed to funnel the oncoming husks. At first, the great wooden walls seemed quite far apart, but they soon grew closer and closer. Any advancing husk foot troops would find themselves packed tighter and tighter together as they lurched toward the squad's shield generator. And then, when they were really squeezed in tight, the squad would pop up—Mikaleh and Janet on one side, and Sam and Sammy on the other— and rain down all manner of things that exploded and went *BOOM!* and made husks disappear.

"Just go," Mikaleh said. "We haven't hit any-body in the crossfire in weeks."

"Yes," Sam said. "But I'm still smarting from the last time. C'mon, Sammy."

The ninja and the outlander scuttled back to their side of the construction—Sammy achiev-ing this through several spectacular jumps—and they settled in for the coming pitcher attack.

The husks advanced slowly. The wait was interminable. Pitchers did not move quickly. Mikaleh decided to take a sniper rifle out of her inventory and start picking them off at a dis-tance. She loaded a round, brought the weapon up, and locked the crosshairs on the rotting fore-head of one of the pitchers at the front.

"Also, who do they even play?"

Mikaleh lowered her weapon.

"What?"

"Like, are they all on one team?" Janet said. "That would be pretty strange, wouldn't it? If you're a baseball team, you want to play against another baseball team. And what about other positions? Pitcher is just one position on the team. If you've got a whole team of pitchers, then who plays third base?"

"Why are you curious about this sort of stuff?" Mikaleh said. "You're as bad as Sam. 'Pitchers throw bones at you if you don't shoot them first.' There. That's the whole field guide to pitchers. Done. That's everything you need to know."

"Hmm, I'm still not sure," Janet said dream-ily, still leaning on her sledgehammer. "What if they have pitching contests? Like, maybe they throw bones to see who can throw the straight-est. That would be fun to watch, at least from a distance."

"Do you mind?" Mikaleh said, raising her sniper rifle once more.

"Be my guest," Janet said with a grin.

Once more, Mikaleh drew her bead on the pitcher in the front of the pack. She let her cross-hairs make a circuit of the creature's moldering body. Would she take it out with a headshot? Traditional, but a bit predictable. She could also shoot it through the chest. Or take out one of its knees—which sent pitchers falling forward in a way that could be very funny. Or what about shooting off its pitching arm entirely? That was another good option. A pitcher without a pitching arm was practically useless. It might still try to bite you, if you got right up next to it, but anybody who did that was sort of asking for it.

Suddenly Mikaleh lowered her weapon.

She blinked twice very hard—as if trying to clear something from her eyes—then raised her weapon and looked again. Then lowered it once more.

"What is *wrong* with you today?" Janet asked. "Just shoot already."

"Something is amiss," Mikaleh said.

"Yes, I know," Janet said. "They've sent all pitchers. We've just been over this."

"No," Mikaleh said, lowering her scope again. "I can see into their satchels with my scope, and they're not carrying bones."

"They're not?" Janet said. "Seriously?"

Before Mikaleh could respond, Janet had produced a sniper rifle of her own and begun looking down the scope. "Ha!" she said. "You're right."

Then an awkward pause.

"But if they're not bones . . ." Janet continued. "What are they?"

Mikaleh was way ahead of her.

"They look like pieces of crumpled-up paper," she replied. "Or maybe paper-mache."

"Oh," said Janet. "Well, that's not a very good projectile. Paper is much softer than bone. It's going to bounce right off us. Quite a misstep by the pitchers, I'd say."

"Yes," Mikaleh said. "But I'm also worried it could be something wrapped in paper."

"Maybe they're explosives!" said Janet. "Sometimes bombs come wrapped in paper."

"Yeah . . ." Mikaleh said thoughtfully. "I was thinking that too. Or firebombs. Or grenades. Lots of options. I just don't know."

"Probably, you should shoot one to see what happens," Janet said. "You know, as a test. If it explodes, we'll know it's some kind of bomb."

"Let's give it a moment more," Mikaleh said. "I want to see what they do."

Mikaleh had learned that the post-Storm world was not always as it first seemed. Things had changed. Ways you might expect things to be orderly and predictable could often suddenly diverge from expected patterns for seemingly no reason. Animals that had once been friendly could now be violent, and vice versa. You just didn't know what was going to surprise you next. These were odd times.

So, as the pitchers marched forward in an orderly line and began to throw their little paper balls, Mikaleh was many things, but "surprised" was not among them.

"Oh my goodness," said Janet. "Those aren't wads of paper at all. They fly much too far."

"They're paper tied around something heavy and hard," Mikaleh responded. "Probably rocks."

"I once tied a message to a rock and threw it at the window of a boy I liked," Janet remembered fondly. "This was back in the 'before-days' of course. Anyhow, I thought his window was open, and it wasn't. It was very embarrassing. Got his attention though."

The pitchers continued to launch their paper-coated missiles. In addition to not throwing bones, the other strange feature of all this—Mikaleh quickly realized—was that the pitchers were completely out of range. Normally a pitcher never threw unless it was in range of hitting you. But today, their lobs were landing several feet short of the outermost wall that Janet had built. And the pitchers did not seem to care.

From their position on the other side of the funnel, Sam and Sammy both stood up, looked at Mikaleh, and gave exaggerated shrugging motions. The message was clear: What gives?

Mikaleh made a lowering motion with her hand, indicating that the pair should be patient.

Then, just when she thought these actions could become no stranger, the pitchers showed Mikaleh they had one more trick up their sleeves. After each pitcher had emptied his or her satchel, they began to back away. Not just a few feet. They started walking backward until they passed into the mist at the edge of the shield projection. Then, one by one, they disappeared.

Husks had been known, in extreme cases, to take evasive action—or what *appeared* to be evasive action but was probably just confusion—yet Mikaleh had never known them to straight-up retreat. Even when outnumbered, outmaneuvered, and outgunned, husks seemed to prefer to fight to the end. Say what you wanted about

them, they were very dedicated to their cause.
(Even if the cause was just eating the brains of
the nearest survivor. Even when the odds were
totally stacked against them, the husks always
took their chances.)

Until now.

In mere moments, the pitchers had retreated
from the field. One by one, they passed into the
emptiness of the Storm beyond.

Mikaleh, Janet, Sam, and Sammy all looked
on in disbelief.

For a long beat, nobody said anything. Janet's
mouth hung open in surprise so long that she
began to drool.

Only the sound of her own drool pooling on
the rampart at her feet jostled her out of her
stupor.

"What the heck was that?" Janet asked.

"I don't know yet," said Mikaleh, jumping
down from her position and carefully advancing
across the field. "But be careful. This could be
some kind of trap."

"Ooh, I hadn't thought of that," said Janet.
"Like maybe those things wrapped in paper
are bombs with timers. And just a few minutes
from now . . . *KA-BLOOEY!* They're all going to
explode."

"That's one possibility, yes," Mikaleh said
seriously.

From the other side of the bulwark, Sam and
Sammy jumped down and joined them. Sammy
reluctantly sheathed his sword, disappointed
that there would be no husks to turn into sushi.
Sam was hastily scribbling field notes in his
notepad.

"This is just incredible!" Sam said. "Completely new behavior. We're literally going to have to rewrite the book on pitchers."

They advanced to within a few feet of the paper wads.

"I'm squad leader, so I should be the one to take this risk," Mikaleh said, and bent down to pick one of the wads up.

"If you're blown to smithereens, I'll record your deeds for posterity," Sam said, indicating his written notes. "But I hope it won't come to that, because I like having you around."

"And I like *being* around," Mikaleh said. "But something tells me this isn't something as simple as a timed bomb."

Mikaleh lifted one of the little wads from the ground. It was a rock wrapped in paper. The paper had been tied on with a string for good measure.

"Hold out your sword," Mikaleh said to Sammy.

In a (literal) flash, the ninja's heavy katana was drawn.

Mikaleh tapped the wrapped rock against it. The blade cut easily through the string, and all the way down to the rock below. She let the string fall to the ground, then began unwrapping the rock.

The rock itself was plain and unremarkable. Mikaleh turned it over in her hand, finding nothing out of the ordinary. But the underside of the paper wrapping, she noticed, was much more interesting.

"It's a message," Mikaleh said.

It was. Though scrawled in a hand so crude it was difficult to read, it was obvious that the paper wrapping contained an intentional communication.

"What does it say?" asked Janet.

Mikaleh narrowed her eyes and tried to read what had been so inexpertly written.

"It's hard to make out, but I think it's trying to say: 'Midnight tonight. Stonewood. By the crooked tree.'"

Mikaleh looked up from the paper.

"How strange."

"Want to hear something stranger?" said Sammy, who had unwrapped a rock of his own. "That's what this one says as well."

"And this one," Sam added. "All the rocks have the same message."

Janet picked up a rock also and took a look.

"You'd think, if they were going to go to all the trouble to do this, they would take the time to work on their collective penmanship," she said. "I mean, what's the point of an invitation if we can't even read it?"

"I think they probably *did* work on this," said Mikaleh. "That's the disturbing thing. Have you ever looked at a husk up close?"

"'Course I have," Janet said. "I've done that thousands of times. Usually, right before I split one in two with an axe or blow it to kingdom come with a great big shotgun."

"If that's true, then you know their eyes are usually half-rotted out of their heads," Mikaleh said.

"Well, yeah," said Janet.

"And what about their hands?" asked Mikaleh.

"What about them?" Janet asked. "They're usually rotten too. Or worn down so they're like an animal's talons. That's one of the things that makes them so dangerous. And gross. I try not to think about husk hands any more than I have to, thank you very much."

"Right, so if you could hardly see, and could hardly hold a pencil, then what do you think it would look like if *you* tried to write a little eight-word message."

"Hmm," Janet said. "Probably like this. Point taken."

"Hey, guys," Sam said. "I'm as interested in husk penmanship as the next man, but right now I'm just a little more interested in *why they've invited us to a meeting in the middle of the night!*"

Mikaleh had to grant that Sam had a point. As remarkable as husk writing was, husks arranging for a meeting was positively unheard of. Mikaleh began to think very carefully about how they ought to proceed.

"It's an odd way of arranging a meeting," Janet said thoughtfully as Mikaleh considered what to do. "Whatever happened to giving some-one a call or sending an email? Actually, I guess those things haven't really been possible since the Storm came. But still."

"Using pitchers makes sense, in a way," said Sam, consulting his notes. "Think about it. If *you* were a husk and you wanted to communicate with a human, how would you do it? Keeping in mind that most humans either run from you, or else try to shoot, stab, or explode you on sight."

"Sometimes I do all of the above," Sammy interjected, "just to keep my bases covered."

"Seriously though," Sam continued. "By the time you've walked up to a human—and most husks walk quite slowly, as I've documented well—the human has either high tailed it, or blown you into little tiny zombie bits. No, I believe a long-range approach, such as the pitchers have deployed, is probably their best option. It's actually quite clever of them. Mikaleh, what do you think?"

Mikaleh seemed lost in thought, but after a moment she spoke.

"I think it could be a trap. I'm trying to think of any way that it's not."

The rest of the squad nodded seriously.

"If we know one thing about husks, it's that they hate humans," she continued. "They're always attacking our shield generators and smashing up everything we build."

"And trying to eat us," said Janet. "That's a big one too."

"Yes," seconded Sammy. "That's probably the one I dislike the most, if I had to choose."

"Yes, they also try to eat us," Mikaleh said. "So I have a hard time believing that something has happened to make them change all that. Until husks stop wanting to smash our stuff and eat us, I have trouble thinking how we could safely meet with them."

"So this invitation *is* a trap," Janet said confidently. "The husks are just seeing if we're dumb enough to fall for it, eh?"

Then Mikaleh said: "Unless . . ."

Janet looked up.

"Unless? Unless what?"

"Well . . ." Mikaleh said. "Sometimes there are things you want, but then there are other things you want even more."

"Sure," Janet said. "I can relate to that. Like I want to be totally buff with zero body fat, but then also I want a pizza *so bad,* om nom nom!"

"You're getting the idea," Mikaleh said.

"I am?" said Janet. "Because mostly now I'm just thinking about pizza."

Mikaleh became very still, as she always did when she was thinking carefully. "What if there's something that husks like even more than eating humans and trashing our stuff?"

The group was at a loss to answer.

"I'll tell you what I think," Mikaleh continued. "If there *were* such a thing, then the husks might look past how delicious we were in order to get it."

"Wow," said Sam. "This is more than even *I* am used to thinking about husk psychology."

"Same here," said Sammy. "Usually I'm just interested thinking about new ways to chop them into tiny pieces."

Mikaleh suddenly had the feeling that a decision of great consequence was before her, and that her choice could have a ripple effect, impacting far more people than her alone. It was the sensation of the future balancing on the edge of a knife.

The war against the husks was—to one way of thinking—going well. Humans were fighting back. They were learning to use weapons and build fortifications. They were expanding their shield domes to new parts of the world, and taking back areas that had once been entirely under husk control. And new survivors were being found every day, and their specialist capabilities were always added to the fight!

But . . .

To another way of thinking, there was much more work still to be done, and things often looked very grim indeed. In all the years since the coming of the Storm, nobody had determined precisely what the Storm even was. Was it man-made—some kind of secret government project gone awry? Was it supernatural? Was it something sent by hostile aliens from another world who sought to terraform the Earth with terrifying zombies—perhaps as a means of preparing it for invasion. (This last hypothesis was Mikaleh's favorite, but only because it was the most dramatic.) In truth, though the surviving humans were learning to band together to fight the husks, no core questions had ever been answered. Very little about the husks was known (despite the extensive work of amateur scientists like Sam). Were the rules going to keep changing from day to day? Were terrifying new forms of husks going to appear? Nobody knew. And anybody who said they did was lying. (Well, probably they were.) Faced with this uncertainty, Mikaleh had a hard time feeling like it was truthful to say that things were going well. In a situation like this, Mikaleh thought, she—or any other human—would be a fool to simply coast on their accomplishments.

"I say we go."

Janet, Sam, and Sammy all looked over at Mikaleh at the same time.

"Huh?" Janet said.

"What about traps?" Sam said.

"Yeah," added Sammy. "Did you somehow think of a way it's *not* a trap?"

"I don't know what it is," Mikaleh said evasively, rising and beginning to pace in a circle. "I just have this feeling that we ought to go. I think we could miss learning something important about the husks if we don't."

Sam seemed to find this unbelievable. He stood and pushed his glasses all the way up his nose.

"A feeling?" he said. "No offense, but this is our safety you're talking about here. I'm more interested in learning about the husks than anybody, but a *feeling* that something isn't a trap isn't the same as a good reason why it's not one."

Then Janet came to Mikaleh's defense.

"Now now," she said. "Remember that time in Plankerton when Mikaleh felt like there were a bunch of survivors under that house . . . and then *there were*? Or that morning outside of the industrial park when she said she 'felt like' we were being watched, and then a bunch of flaming skulls started raining down on us because some lobbers were totally watching us?"

"So?" said Sam. "Those could be coincidences. Give me one logical reason why we should go tonight and put ourselves in danger."

Suddenly, Mikaleh stopped walking in a circle. She had turned away, but now she turned back to face the group.

"I'll give you a reason," she said. "And it's not because I have a 'feeling.' It's because for all of those pages of notes you've taken on husks, you still don't know where they came from. You still don't know what they are, not really. And you still don't know exactly what we have to do in order to get rid of them for good. One of the most important parts of problem-solving is being curious. It's the only way you learn new things. Tell me, Sam, aren't you curious? Don't you want to learn more?"

"Of course I do," he said without hesitation. "It's the 'getting ambushed by husks' part that I'm concerned about."

"I'll tell you what," Mikaleh said. "You'll have all afternoon—and the first part of the evening— to think of a counter-trap."

Sam looked left and right, and then left again. "Is that like a thing that triggers a trap, so it closes on the person who set it?"

"Could be," Mikaleh said with a smile. "Or it could be anything else you devise that will help us out if the husks *do* spring a trap on us. You can plan a way to ambush the ambushers, so to speak."

"Huh," Sam said, the gears in his head slowly beginning to turn. "I think I can do that. A trap to trap people who are laying a trap? Interesting . . . maybe if I can get back to base and begin drawing up some schematics . . ."

"Good idea," Mikaleh said. "In fact, why don't we all head back to base right now to prepare. But first, let's burn these notes and throw these rocks back into the forest. We don't want anybody else stumbling on to them and getting ideas. We wouldn't want curious strangers to interrupt our midnight meeting."

"Oh absolutely not," Sam said. "Introducing another variable like that would totally mess up my plans to trap the trappers with a trap. It would become . . . far too complicated."

After they had made a small campfire and burned the poorly scrawled notes, they headed back in the direction of their home shield base.

"Psst," Janet said as she walked beside Mikaleh. "Good thinking with that counter-trap business."

Mikaleh nodded. Both women glanced behind to where Sam still seemed to be lost in thought, jotting plans for some kind of device into his notebook while Sammy looked on.

"It will be a good way to keep his mind occupied until midnight," Mikaleh said. "And who knows. He might actually come up with something useful. Stranger things have happened."

CHAPTER TWO

There were several crooked trees in Stonewood, but even in the blackest dark of midnight, Mikaleh knew which one was the most crooked. And it was there that she guided her squad.

Several yards off from the crooked tree, a lone outcropping in the landscape jutted up into the sky.

"We should stop here," Sam said.

Mikaleh looked at her watch. It was 11:55.

"That is, Sammy and I should," Sam quickly clarified. "The two of you should go ahead to the meeting at the tree. But this is where I'm going to set up our counter-trap . . . to the trap you're almost certainly walking into."

Mikaleh was also curious. "What exactly are you planning?" she asked. "To be honest, I wasn't sure you were actually going to come up with anything."

Sam's expression said he would not take her lack of confidence personally.

"I'm going to build a rampart with an epic wall trap," Sam explained. "A wall launcher, to be precise."

"But how are you going to launch a husk if it ambushes us way over by that tree?" Janet asked.

"I'm not going to launch it; I'm going to launch *us*," Sam said proudly. "I can work the trajectory so that at the first sign of trouble, I can send Sammy careening through the air right on top of you. He'll basically be a flurry of flying blades, and they won't be expecting it."

"I'll be careful only to be a flurry toward the husks, and not at either of you," Sammy said helpfully.

"Given the distance to cover and the wind-speed tonight, I think we'll be able to come to your rescue in about five seconds," Sam said, then added: "Ten tops."

"Who says we're going to need rescuing?" Janet asked defensively. "If anybody will need to be rescued, it'll be some husks being rescued from *us*."

"Whoa now," Mikaleh said, stepping between Janet and Sam. "I'm sure we're going to be just fine. But look at the time. We need to get going. C'mon."

As Sam and Sammy began to craft their epic wall launcher, Mikaleh and Janet crept the rest of the way to the old crooked tree. They reached the ancient twisting hulk of timber and stood before it. The tree was long dead but still looked eerily like a coiled animal that might spring to life at any moment.

"I don't see why somebody hasn't chopped this old thing up for planks yet," said Janet as they milled about in the moonlight beside it.

"Probably because it looks like it would start yelling at you if you did," said Mikaleh. "Or else reach back with one of its branches and punch you in the face."

Janet looked again at the strange old tree, then nodded to say Mikaleh's diagnosis was not unreasonable.

There was nobody around. Certainly, there were no husks to see. The wind seemed to whip up and change direction every few minutes, but Mikaleh found that she couldn't smell any husks either. (It was hard for her to articulate exactly what a husk smelled like, but none of the adjectives would have been anything good. Husk were about fifteen different shades of gross.)

Mikaleh and Janet both appeared to be unarmed—which was to say their hands were, for the moment, empty . . . though both carried a veritable arsenal concealed under their coats.

Mikaleh looked back over her shoulder to where Sam and Sammy waited atop the small fort they had quickly built. She could not see in the shadows, but knew that Sam was almost definitely observing her through the scope of a sniper rifle. She gave him a little wave. In the distance, a flashlight blinked twice in quick succession, acknowledging her.

Mikaleh and Janet looked at the tree again, then at each other.

"How long do we wait?" Janet asked.

"Let's give it a few minutes longer," Mikaleh said. "We've come all this way."

"Hey, I just thought of something else," Janet said. "What if this is a trick by the husks, but not to eat us. What if they want to distract us? Like while we're out in middle-of-nowhere Stonewood, they're ransacking our base?"

Mikaleh shrugged. "There are other survivors at our base who could hold them off," she said.

"Yeah," said Janet. "But they're not as good at killing husks as we are."

"Well, of course not," Mikaleh said. "Nobody's as good at killing husks as we are."

Both young women smiled. Then Janet frowned. Yet another possibility had occurred to her.

"Sayyyy," she began. "You don't suppose that, somehow, it's *the tree* that we're supposed to speak with?"

No sooner than these words had left Janet's mouth, a horrible stench diffused around them. The smell of something being revealed from underground. Something old and stinky and horrible.

Then a voice said: "Don't be silly. Trees can't talk."

Mikaleh and Janet both spun around on their heels. Their hands reached instinctively for their weapons. And far in the distance, at the edge of hearing, Mikaleh thought she could just detect the noise of a bolt being drawn back on a sniper rifle.

Before them stood a husk. There was nothing remarkable about him. He actually seemed a bit on the smaller side. His neck was twisted at a strange, unnatural angle. It was clear that it had been hiding underneath the ground, and had only just burrowed up to the surface.

It looked back and forth between Mikaleh and Janet, but did not appear aggressive.

"I said that trees can't talk," said the husk.

"Until a moment ago, I didn't think husks could either," said Mikaleh.

The husk shrugged. (Given the angle of its neck, this was quite a feat.)

"It's not that we can't," it said. "It's that most of the time we don't want to. Human speech sounds so ridiculous. You know how we sound to you?"

"Yeah," said Mikaleh. "Like a bunch of stupid weird groaning."

"Then that's probably how you sound to us," it said.

Mikaleh saw the husk's point. "I'm thinking something important must be going on for you to ask us here like this," Mikaleh said.

The husk nodded cautiously.

"And it's so important you're even restraining yourself from trying to eat us," Mikaleh continued.

"Yes," said the husk. "You will never appreciate the amount of self-control I am using right now. Both of you smell absolutely delicious."

"So, do you want to cut to the chase and tell us what we're doing here?" Mikaleh said. "Or should I start guessing?"

"I don't know if husks understand sarcasm," Janet interjected. "But that was sarcasm. So we're not going to keep guessing. You're just going to tell us right now. *Or else.*"

Janet put her hands on her hips and leaned forward sternly. She towered over the diminutive husk. It looked as though, if she's wanted to, she could have ripped him in half with her bare hands.

Mikaleh thought she saw the husk beginning to tremble.

"It's just . . . uh . . . we asked you here . . . uh . . . because we've lost something," the husk said.

"Lost something?" said Mikaleh.

"Yes," the husk said, nodding hastily.

"And what makes you think we're the ones to find it . . . whatever it is?" said Janet.

"Are you kidding?" said the husk. "Your squad has shot, exploded, and carved up more husks than any four humans left in the world. We send our best people up against you, and we still lose, every time. You guys know how to get things done. And you also . . . I'll just say it. You just kick butt. It's as simple as that."

"I never thought I'd say this to a husk," Janet said. "But you know how to get on my good side."

"I'm glad you like what you're hearing," the husk replied.

"What is the thing you lost?" Mikaleh asked.

"This might sound stupid," the husk began. "But it's a key. A very special one. It's a gold key with a red ruby handle. We think one of the mist monsters took it. A smasher named Grumpy Joe. He's very large and very mean. He lives in a grotto out past the grasslands. We were hoping you could go find him and get it back for us."

"Wait, wait, wait," said Janet, waving her hand in the air as if to dispel an invisible pall that had been cast. "Aren't you guys all on the same side? Don't all of you know each other, and so forth?"

"Not at all," said the husks. "Do you know all humans?"

"Of course not," said Janet. "That would be weird."

"Well, there you go," said the husk. "I'm not friends with every mist monster. And I don't actually know many husks. In fact, when I say 'we' would like you to find this key, it's really just a small group of us husks. A handful. Okay, mostly just me."

"But all those pitchers who threw those rocks with your message wrapped around them—" Janet began.

"We used hired guns," said the husk. "They didn't even know what they were throwing. We told them it was stink bombs. And pitchers never ask that many questions to begin with. In fact, any husks you see in the course of this errand are almost definitely not going to know what is going on."

"So that's why you're not asking other husks for help," Janet said, proud at having deduced this. "You're trying to keep it a secret that you've lost this key. Or that a smasher took it. Or whatever."

The husk did not immediately respond.

It was then that Janet noticed how quiet Mikaleh had suddenly become. When Janet glanced over, Mikaleh pulled her aside.

"Janet, I think we need to go over here, to the other side of the tree, and talk for a second," said Mikaleh.

"Are you serious?" Janet said. "What can you have to say that you can't say in front of a husk? I've said all kind of embarrassing things in front of husks over the years, but mostly because I didn't think they could understand me. Hey—"

Without further ado, Mikaleh grabbed Janet hard by her wrist and pulled her around to the other side of the tree. The husk just looked on, plainly not in a hurry to get anywhere.

"Janet," Mikaleh whisper-shouted. "Do you remember in the very first days after the Storm came—when we were still building our first base, making tools into improvised weapons, and still trying to figure out what was going on? People came and went back then, and survivors often didn't know if they could trust each other. But do you remember there was an old man in a long gray overcoat who used to come by. He was something of a crazy old storyteller, or so everybody thought. People used to just call him 'The Traveler.' Remember?"

"Eh, sort of," said Janet. "There were a lot of weird old hobos who came through back then. And they were always saying weird things."

"This one used to talk about a gold key sometimes," Mikaleh said urgently. "A gold key *with a ruby handle*. And it was somehow connected to his main point—the thing he was always babbling about—the Last Survivor. Remember?"

"Again, sort of," said Janet. "But sort of not."

"He used to say that there was a Last Survivor waiting to be found somewhere," Mikaleh said.

"Yeah, but all survivors are lost before we find them, if you think about it," said Janet.

"But this survivor was extra-special," Mikaleh said. "Finding him . . . or her . . . or it . . . would give you a tremendous power that he thought would make the difference in the fight against the husks."

"Well, that sounds good," said Janet.

"Uh-huh," Mikaleh agreed. "And the Traveler always used to say that the first clue to finding this Last Survivor would be a gold key. With a ruby handle."

"Oh," said Janet. "Well, that *is* kind of interesting now. Back then, I thought that guy was just a crazy hobo."

"So did I," said Mikaleh. "Until now."

"But wait," said Janet. "If the key is connected to the Last Survivor . . . and the Last Survivor gives you power to fight against the husks . . . then why do the husks want the key connected to it?"

"Maybe they're trying to make sure we don't get it first," Mikaleh said.

"Oh!" said Janet. "That *would* make sense. Those sneaky devils."

Mikaleh and Janet peered over at the husk, who appeared to be waiting patiently.

"I think this is worth looking into further," Mikaleh said. "But I also think we're not getting the whole story yet. Whatever we do, I don't think we should let the husk know about the Last Survivor."

"I'll follow your lead," said Janet.

They walked back to where the husk was shifting back and forth idly from foot to foot.

"So?" said the husk. "What have you decided? Will you help me and my friends retrieve our special key from that mean old smasher?"

"Why should we help you?" ask Mikaleh. "You haven't said anything about payment."

For the first time, the husk smiled. It was an unnerving sight. Most of its cheeks and teeth were missing.

"I have a special prize in mind," said the husk. "Treasure. Treasure beyond your wildest imaginings."

"If you haven't noticed, we're kind of in the middle of a zombie apocalypse right now," Mikaleh said. "A chest full of gold and jewels isn't really as valuable to us as, say, building materials, food, and BluGlo would be."

"Who says it's not building materials and food and BluGlo," said the husk. "'Treasure' is an abstract idea. Almost anything can be considered treasure in the right circumstances."

"He's got you there," said Janet brightly.

Mikaleh rolled her eyes. "Then I have just one more question," she said. "Why?"

"Why?" hissed the husk. "Why what?"

"Why do you want this key back? What's it open? Why is it, you know, important to you?"

The husk pulled back its head like a snake. It shuffled and hesitated. It was clear to Mikaleh that it did not want to answer.

Finally, it said: "If someone took something that belonged to you, wouldn't *you* want it back?"

"Well, sure," said Mikaleh. "But I'd have to want it really, *really* bad to go and hire a squad of my sworn enemies to go and get it for me."

The husk hesitated once more.

"We want it back because it was stolen from us," it said. "I can tell you nothing more. Take it or leave it."

Mikaleh and Janet made a show of looking at each other as though the matter involved deep consideration. Eventually, they appeared to relent.

"Okay," Mikaleh said. "I can't believe I'm agreeing to work with a husk, but yes. We'll do it."

"Yeah," Janet added. "We'll go to that grotto and look for that smasher. How hard could it be?"

"I'm sure not hard at all for brave warriors like yourselves," said the husk.

"How will we find you once we've obtained the key?" Mikaleh asked.

"Hmm," said the husk, as though this had not occurred to him. "I can't have you bringing it to me, as that would defeat the purpose of making this a secret mission. Also, humans who go into the Storm have a weird habit of dying. Since this is the case, let's agree to meet here in one week. By the tree. At midnight. I assume one week will be enough time for you to get the job done?"

"Heh, I'll bet we'll have it twenty-four hours from now!" boasted Janet.

"Then you'll just have to find a way to pass the other six days," the husk said.

As if their meeting were finished, the husk turned to go. Mikaleh noticed that he had a strange hobble when he walked.

"One more second," Mikaleh called.

"Yes?" said the husk.

"What's your name?"

The husk seemed to consider it for a moment. Perhaps husks had no names, and she had touched upon a sore point.

"Oh, sorry," she said, hardly believing she was apologizing to a husk. "Do you not have names?"

"*Not have names!*" the husk said, shaken from his silence by the ignorance of her question. "Husks have long, complicated, deeply meaningful names! We have rich inner lives that you humans know nothing about. And you never bother to ask. You just shoot us in the face the moment you see us!"

"In most of those cases, you are trying to eat us," Janet pointed out.

"So yes, I have a name," the husk said defensively. "But considering that I'm trying to keep this very hush-hush, maybe we shouldn't use them."

"Fine," said Janet, "but just so you know, we'll need to talk about you some way. So we'll probably end up giving you a silly nickname you won't like."

"Whatever!" said the husk. "I don't care."

"I'm thinking 'Droopy' would be good," Janet continued, "because of the crazy way your spine and neck droop forward. It's quite unnatural. For a human, anyway."

The husk gave Janet a testy look—during which his spine, neck, and head *did* droop forward most irregularly—and shuffled away into the night. Mikaleh and Janet silently watched him go.

When Droopy had fully disappeared into the darkness, Janet turned to Mikaleh.

"Well, that was . . . Wait. Do you hear something?"

A moment later, the sound Janet heard became very clear indeed. It was the sound of a young man screaming at the top of his lungs. And it was growing louder by the second.

"yeeeeeeeeeeee*AAAAAAAAAAAHHHHHHHH-HHH!*"

The sound concluded with a loud *THUMP* as Sam was catapulted against the side of the crooked tree, about halfway up, and slowly slid down.

In the distance, Mikaleh could see Sammy running after him.

Sam seemed slightly dazed but mostly unhurt. He rose to his feet and dusted himself off. "Sorry about that," he said. "I know the husk is gone. I just figured if we were going to go to so much trouble to build that launcher, it'd be a shame not to use it at least once."

"I know how you feel," Janet said sympathetically. "Whenever we're defending a base, and I spend all this time building the best walls, and bulwarks, and funnels—and then the monsters don't even bother to attack from that direction? It makes me so furious."

Mikaleh looked at Sam doubtfully, then up at the spot he'd left on the tree where he'd smacked into it. "*That* was your plan in case this was an ambush?" she asked playfully.

"Hey, my trajectory might have been slightly off, but I got here quick, didn't I?" Sam said.

"Yeah," confirmed Sammy, who arrived huffing and puffing from his run. "That was way faster than trying to sprint it."

"What did the husk say?" Sam asked.

Mikaleh gave the twins a quick version of what had happened.

"I can't believe it!" Sam said when she had finished.

"I know, right?" Mikaleh said. "It's pretty unbelievable. I thought the Last Survivor was just a legend told by a crazy man who used to hang out around our base. But now that it could actually be real—"

"You *talked* to a *husk*?" Sam said. "This literally rewrites the book on what we thought we knew about them. Seriously, I'm going to have to throw away all of my notes and start fresh!"

Sammy, unencumbered by years of field research, brought a new perspective.

"It sounds like this is going to be very dangerous, even for something *we* do. And we do a lot of dangerous things! Best case scenario, we have to fight a mist monster on home turf. Worst case scenario . . . I don't even like to think about it. Also, maybe this is still a trap."

"Still a trap?" Janet said skeptically. "If some husks were going to trap us, I think they would have done so right here. Tonight."

"I'm not sure about that," said Sammy nervously. "Getting us to go down into a grotto to fight a smasher sounds like bad news. What if they roll a big rock over the entrance after we go in? We could be trapped in there with a smasher. I mean, I'll survive the longest because of my evasive-ninja jumping skills. But I'm afraid the rest of you might be done for. And I say that as a friend."

"I'm glad that I can trust you always to have my best interests in mind," Mikaleh said.

"This all seems a bit strange to me," said Janet. "But then again, it's the most interesting thing that's happened in a while."

"You're not suggesting we go and fight with a smasher for no good reason," said Sammy, who still seemed anxious.

"Oh, smashers aren't that bad," Janet countered. "Just hit 'em with a few RPGs and they go down flat on the ground. *KA-BOOM!*"

Sammy did not seem convinced.

"That what a lot of overconfident people say right before they get beaten to a pulp by a smasher," Sammy said.

"Well, what are you suggesting?" said Janet. "That we don't investigate this more?"

"We don't have to," said Sammy.

"Yes, we do."

They all turned and looked. It was Mikaleh who had spoken.

"Even though it's weird and risky, we have to do it," she continued. "And it's not because of the 'treasure' the husks are offering us, which I don't think even exists. And it's not because we have to prove to anybody that we're tough. It's because this is the first time since the Storm came that I've really had anything like a feeling of hope."

The rest of the squad became serious. Their faces fell. It was rare that Mikaleh addressed them in serious tones. (Normally, one of the great things about working was that she was always so relaxed. It made her a very effective squad leader, at least in the eyes of her followers.) The rest of the squad knew something special was happening.

She continued. "Since all this happened—since the Storm came and the husks were unleashed and we became like refugees in a world that used to be ours—I haven't had a whole lot of hope. I mean sure, we have good days and we have bad days. And my days have collectively gotten a whole lot better since the three of you became my squad. But it's a sliding scale. Remember how things used to be before all of this? Before anybody had to be a constructor or a ninja or an outlander?"

"Hey, I was always actually a ninja," Sammy said. "I mean, I took classes down at the Y and had cool ninja swords hanging on my wall and everything."

"It wasn't like your *job*-job though," Janet interjected. "You worked at a frozen yogurt stand."

"That's kind of my point," Mikaleh said. "Imagine your best day here. Your best day in . . . whatever you want to call our existence now. Imagine you chopped so many husk heads that you lost count."

"That would be a lot," Sammy said. "I can count pretty high."

"Okay," Mikaleh said. "But then imagine just an average day in your life before. You worked at the frozen yogurt stand. You came home and had dinner with Sam and fought about what to watch on TV, and then maybe practiced some sword moves. You did all that in a world without husks. You did all that in a world with reliable electricity. Heat in the winter and air conditioning in the summer. And your friends and family."

Sammy's face fell. It was clear that he did remember and miss those things.

"I would probably trade the best day I ever had after the Storm came for an average day back like it was before," he said.

"Me too," said Janet.

"Me three," added Sam. "Writing a book about husks is satisfying, but not as satisfying as imagining husks didn't ever exist in the first place."

Mikaleh nodded, pleased that her squad was in alignment. "Hearing about something that might be connected to the Last Survivor—even though I don't really know what it is—is enough to make me feel like it might be possible to get back to the old days again. The way things used to be before all of this nonsense started. And if there's even a chance this could be a step toward making the world more like it used to be again, then I want to take it. We have to do more than survive. We have to get rid of these husks once and for all. We have to make the world ours again. And I want us to take any step we can in that direction."

"We're with you," said Janet. "Even if it means going into scary grottos and beating the heck out of enormous smashers until they give us a key back."

"Good," said Mikaleh, "because I think it does."

CHAPTER THREE

The grasslands were probably the the most placid part of the known world that had been left after the rise of the husks and the coming of the Storm. It was full of trees that could be chopped for wood, and rocks that could likewise be harvested for building materials. It was also riddled with mines and mysterious tunnels where you could find metal and other useful things. Sometimes crates of ammunition had been stocked there, and sometimes you ran into friendly survivors who were always happy to see a friendly face.

The problem with such a place, by Mikaleh's reckoning at least, was that it was the kind of a place where you could get lulled into a false sense of security and safety.

And then suddenly a bunch of husks came pouring out of nowhere and you were still fumbling for your shotgun while they overran your position.

Mikaleh did her best to stay sharp. So did the rest of her squad.

After a good night's sleep back in their base, they had set off for the grasslands first thing. The morning was calm and still. The gentlest of breezes stirred the grass underneath their feet.

Mikaleh seemed to have a rough idea of the grotto's location. As the rest of the squad followed her, they passed small houses and shacks left over from the time before the Storm.

"What do you think these were?" Janet said. "Hunting cabins? Vacation huts? Sheds for storing equipment?"

"Back up," Mikaleh said. "Who ever heard of a vacation *hut*?"

"Well, maybe you can't afford much more than a hut, but you still know it's important to take a relaxing vacation from time to time," answered Janet. "So, you know, you make do."

"I guess so," said Mikaleh.

"This part of the world just seems to be full of these little one-room shacks," Janet mused. "I just wonder where they all came from. But it's a good thing they're here. If husks pop up, you can suddenly jump inside and close the door to plan your next move. And if you know the husks are coming, you can use them as a starting point for building some defensive positions of your own. It's a pretty good system, I suppose. And the workmanship is so good! These old buildings are very tough. Of course . . . I expect it's much easier to do high-quality workmanship when you aren't worried about murderous zombies attacking you. Being in a race against time with the undead has a way of convincing even the best constructors to cut a corner now and then."

"Speaking of corners, the way to the grotto is just around the corner of that outcropping up ahead," said Sam. "What are you thinking when it comes to taking down this smasher? RPG? Some kind of TNT explosion?"

"I was thinking more . . . words," said Mikaleh.

Sam looked as though he had not heard her correctly.

"Did you say . . . words?"

Mikaleh nodded.

"Our goal here is not just to get this gold key with a ruby handle," she said. "It's also to figure out exactly what's going on. Try to be as curious about smashers as you are about regular husks."

Sam made a noise like a disagreeing horse.

"But husks are so much more interesting!" he protested. "They're everywhere. There are always a lot of them. They're the most numerous creature that comes out of the Storm, and therefore—in my opinion—the most successful. Despite being missing eyes and limbs and other parts, they still find a way to be quite a formidable foe. And while appearing to be entirely oblivious to one another, they end up attacking in a coordinated way that looks an awful lot like teamwork. I know they're the enemy, but I never stop being impressed by them."

"And I'm guessing you'll have less to say about smashers," Mikaleh said with a grin.

"You guess right," Sam announced in a tone that said this should be obvious. "They're big and they have a big hand and they smash stuff. Case closed. What more's there to say?"

Mikaleh had the feeling that there was actually a lot more to say, but she knew Sam was not going to be receptive to a discussion at the moment. If their knowledge of smashers paled in comparison to what they knew of husks, it was only because they were so rare, and when they took the battlefield, they were almost immediately the target of everyone's fire. They didn't usually last long enough to be observed very much.

The squad began to make their way around the outcropping.

"Look," Sam said to Mikaleh, "you can use all the words you want; I'm just going to have an RPG ready to fire just in case."

Janet said: "I think that's as much of a compromise as you're going to get from him, Mikaleh."

Mikaleh smiled. "In that case, I suppose I ought to take it," she said.

On the other side of the outcropping was indeed the grotto . . . or the entrance to it. The ground opened into a series of crudely cut earthen stairs—sized so that a smasher might have no trouble walking up and down them. The stairs led down to a dark pit that seemed to go on forever. In the distance, they could hear the sound of water lapping softly. It smelled like a swamp.

"Err, I was embarrassed to ask before," Janet said, peering doubtfully into the dark recesses of the opening. "But, what's a grotto? I was never totally clear."

"Think of a cave with water in it," Sam said helpfully.

"Okay, I'm thinking of it," Janet said. "What happens now?"

"Nothing happens!" said Sam. "That's what a grotto is. A cave with some water. It can be deep or it can be shallow. That depends on the grotto."

Sammy stepped forward and cupped his ear. "It sounds like this one's got a whole bunch of water," he declared.

"Yes," said Mikaleh. "I've heard of this grotto before—and vaguely of Grumpy Joe—but I've never been inside. It offers no tactical advantage, and there's never been word of anything useful being found inside. Then again, I don't think many folks have got far enough past Grumpy Joe to take a look."

It was not possible—technically speaking— to "cock" an RPG, but Sam managed to make a show that said the weapon on his shoulder was very much prepared to fire.

"Remember," Mikaleh said, "words first. Then rockets."

"Fine," said Sam. "But if some of those words are 'Omigosh, why didn't we just immediately fire the RPG when the smasher came into view?' don't come crying to me."

They began to make their way down the very large steps that descended into darkness.

"I smell something new," Janet said as they grew closer to the opening.

She was known to have the keenest nose in the entire squad. Mikaleh thought this probably correlated to Janet being recognized as the hungriest person in the squad as well. If there was a pie on a windowsill a mile away, or even just some leftovers somebody had forgotten to throw out, Janet always smelled it way before anyone else did.

"What is it?" Mikaleh asked the constructor. "I only smell water."

Janet's face showed she was still processing the odor. They descended farther into the cavernous opening.

"It smells like . . . after a battle," she said.

Mikaleh was not sure what this meant.

"Whatever it is," Janet continued, "it reminds me of when the fighting has just concluded, and Sammy has just beheaded the last husk with his sword, and the head is maybe still rolling across the ground a little, but there's nobody left to fight. That smell. Huh. It's funny. I never thought of that having a smell before. Weird."

They traversed another giant step and passed into the grotto proper. The rock ceiling blotted out the sun. The sound of rushing water was increasingly loud.

"I'm gonna try talking to it," Mikaleh announced. "I don't see Grumpy Joe, but this grotto's not supposed to be very large. I'm sure he'll hear me if I shout."

The rest of the squad readied their weapons.

"Hey!!!" Mikaleh cried as loudly as she could. "Grumpy Joe! Can you come out and talk to us? We just found out that husks can talk, so maybe mist monsters can too! Do you want to come out and say hello?"

There was nothing. No response. Mikaleh's words reverberated off the grotto's walls, but nothing came back in return.

Sam held his RPG tight. They walked a little deeper inside.

Suddenly, Mikaleh stopped dead in her tracks. The rest of the squad stopped too.

Mikaleh whispered: "It's blood."

"What?" said Janet, also keeping her voice low.

The squad looked around in alarm.

"The smell you're smelling," Mikaleh said. "It's blood. Or whatever the goo is that oozes around inside of husks and mist monsters. That's why it reminds you of the smell of after a battle."

The squad sniffed the air.

"Hey, Mikaleh's right!" Sammy said, just a little too loudly. "That *is* the way it smells when I take the head off a husk with a swipe of my sword."

"Yes," Mikaleh said. "And usually when we're through fighting, the ground is soaked with it."

"Wow," said Janet. "I'm always boasting about how good my nose is, but apparently you have a good nose too."

"I'm not just using my nose," Mikaleh said ominously. "Look over there against the wall. You can see it too."

The squad cautiously approached the location Mikaleh had indicated. Turning on their flashlights, they inspected the spot. Sure enough, there were signs that a great battle had occurred. Husks left behind very little after they expired—usually just a few tiny traces of bone or wisps of clothing. The rest evaporated by means still not entirely understood. But if a large enough battle happened—and you knew what to look for—it was possible to get a sense of where husk-based conflicts had occurred. And it was clear, from the detritus that littered the ground, that quite a tussle had happened here.

The squad got down on their haunches and carefully began to sift through the pieces.

Janet found something interesting between the splinters of bone and bits of husk-goo.

"What's this?" she said, holding up a sliver of something hard. "It's like wicker. Got a sort of hexagon shape in parts."

"That's honeycomb," Mikaleh said. "These were beehives. At least some of them were."

"Did you ever hear of beehives being in this cave?" asked Janet.

"No," said Mikaleh. "Just the smasher."

"This just gets stranger and stranger," said Sam. "And not in an interesting way. More like a way that makes it feel like I have butterflies in my stomach all of a sudden."

They sifted through the remaining detritus. It was much the same. Whatever had happened here, the destruction of quite a few beehives had been involved.

"There's one good thing," Janet said, rising back to her feet. "And that's that I don't see anything a human might have left behind. Whatever squad did this were great shots, and it looks like they didn't lose a man. Or woman."

"I'm not so certain it was a squad," Mikaleh said.

"Oh no," said Janet. "What now?"

Mikaleh shined her flashlight farther into the grotto. There, right beside a burbling creek, a strange outline had been pressed into the soft mud of the creek bed. The shape was decidedly humanoid, but it was more than twice the height of a normal person. Maybe three times. It also lacked the symmetry common in most humans. While one of its arms was proportional to a regular person's, the other terminated in a massive distended club bigger than its own torso.

The squad crept close to the outline.

"RIP Grumpy Joe," said Sammy. "And I never got to find out why people said he was grumpy. Probably it was the smashing."

"Probably," Mikaleh said, kneeling down to inspect the outline more closely.

"We'd never have known what happened to him if he'd fallen anyplace other than this mushy mud," Sam observed. "It really held his shape!"

"And look at this," Mikaleh said, pulling a splinter with hexagonal designs up out of the imprint. "Honeycomb here too."

"Wow," said Sammy. "It must have been a very capable squad that came here and defeated Grumpy Joe, and then all of these beehives to boot. Very capable indeed. We'd better watch our backs; another squad is gunning for the top spot."

"I don't think we need to have any concerns about another squad getting a better reputation than us," Mikaleh said, letting the shred of honeycomb fall back down to the grotto floor. "A squad didn't do this. Can't you see? They fought each other."

Sam, Sammy, and Janet all took turns exchanging glances.

"They did?" Sammy said.

"It would explain why there are no bullet holes or shell casings or sword marks on the walls," said Sam.

"First, pitchers pitching strange messages, then a husk that wants to talk to us, and now this," Sammy said. "This is getting stranger all the time."

"Why would beehives fight against a smasher?" Janet asked.

"Maybe it had something they wanted," Mikaleh said.

"The golden key with the ruby handle!" Janet said.

Mikaleh only nodded.

"Maybe it's around here somewhere," Sam suggested.

"We can always check," said Mikaleh. "At any rate, I don't think we're going to encounter any more husks or mist monsters down here. You can probably put away your RPG."

"Eh, I'll think about it," Sam said, leaving the weapon on his shoulder for the moment.

The squad fanned out and began to explore the grotto. There were signs of it being a very lived-in place. Lived in by a smasher, at any rate. Rocks had been pulverized wherever they hung down or stuck up out of the earth. In the back of the grotto, Sammy found a pile of ancient dusty bones. The squad was unable to tell if they were human or animal (or some mixture) but Mikaleh opined that it probably represented the remnants of unlucky creatures that had had the misfortune to wander down into the grotto unarmed.

The squad turned over every moss-covered rock and searched every ledge and nook in the rock walls, but they found no sign of a gold key with a ruby handle.

"How big's the key?" Sammy asked as their search concluded.

"Droopy didn't say," Janet related. "I expect that it's, you know, key-sized."

"I almost have trouble remembering what that is," Sammy confided. "Back before the Storm, I used to use keys all the time. I had a key for my car, and for the house, and for the shed in back. Now it's hardly worth locking up anything at all. Plus, everybody's armed to the teeth, which makes stealing anything a distinctly riskier proposition."

"Well, it's small," Janet said. "Not much bigger than your finger."

"Oh," said Sammy. "Well, I definitely didn't see anything like that."

As Mikaleh completed her searching of the grotto, a strange expression crossed her face. It said that perhaps all was not as it seemed.

"I'm starting to get the distinct feeling that someone was here before us," she said. "It's just not dirty and dusty enough for a grotto where a smasher lived alone. I think somebody was already here, and they already searched this place."

"The beehives!" Janet said. "So *they* have the key?"

"It's a distinct possibility," Mikaleh said.

"This is just getting stranger and stranger," Janet said.

Mikaleh tried to think.

"When we spoke to Droopy last night, he seemed to think the key was here with Grumpy Joe. I think he was telling us the truth. By which I mean, he *believed* that it was true. So I think if beehives came and took the key, they did it very recently. Like *very* recently."

Suddenly, Mikaleh started running. She headed back to the mouth of the grotto.

"Come on!" she said. "I know what we need to do."

CHAPTER FOUR

T his is ridiculous," said Sammy.

"No it's not," said Janet. "And besides, do you have a better idea?"

"Well . . . no," said Sammy. "But that doesn't mean this isn't still ridiculous."

"Quiet, both of you!" Sam said. "Half of trying to find a bee is listening for the buzz."

The squad stood in the clearing near the steps leading down to the grotto. It had occurred to Mikaleh that the thing about beehives was that they tended to leave a few bees behind. They were tiny, but you noticed them if you remembered to look.

"There!" Sam said, then just as quickly added: "No, wait. Darn. That's a fly. No, wait. Maybe it's a bee? No. Definitely a fly."

"Let's spread out in different directions," said Mikaleh. "Give a whistle if you hear anything."

The squad headed off to the four corners of the clearing. Mikaleh made for a rocky outcropping jutting up out of the landscape to the west. She didn't see any bees around it, but she thought she'd better climb to the top to make sure. She began jumping up onto the side of it, trying to scale the face—which only sometimes worked. But after just a few hops, her ears pricked up.

She stopped and turned back around. Her other three squad members were already out of sight.

"Was that someone whistling?" Mikaleh called. "Hellooooo? Did one of you just whistle?"

As Mikaleh listened, the sound she had heard before came again. It was distant, and it *might* have been a whistle. It was low and reedy and soft.

"Look, you need to whistle loud," Mikaleh said. "If you see the bee, do a loud one with both fingers. Please. Otherwise, I can't tell where you are."

The sound came again. It was still strange and low, like the whistler wasn't trying very hard.

"Are you serious?" Mikaleh said. "That's really the best you can do?"

"It's not me!" a voice suddenly cried out.

"And it's not me either!" cried another, nearly identical voice.

From opposite directions, Sam and Sammy made their ways back into the clearing at the mouth of the grotto.

"Was Janet too embarrassed to tell us she's bad at whistling?" Mikaleh asked as the trio began jogging in the direction their constructor had gone. "She shouldn't have been. I'm very understanding."

The sound came again. Slightly louder now but still very soft. The whistle had a warbling to it.

"There!" said Sam, pointing to a cluster of flowers atop a hill on the horizon. "Bees like flowers. She's got to be over there."

They raced toward the hill. Soon they encountered flowers—red and pink and yellow, and they grew knee-high.

The sound came again. It was definitely a whistle. Or, at least, an attempt at one.

Mikaleh crossed the top of the hill. On the other side, sure enough, she found Janet. The constructor was acting very oddly. She was standing stock still, as if impersonating a mannequin. At the same time, she was trying to whistle very quietly. As Mikaleh and the Sams approached, Janet began to rotate very slowly toward them.

"Janet," Mikaleh said, "what on earth are you—"

But then she saw.

One of the fattest, hairiest bumblebees Mikaleh had ever laid eyes on was perched on the very tip of Janet's nose.

"I'm allergic," Janet whispered nervously. "Can you help?"

"You should have said something," Mikaleh replied as she cautiously approached.

"Normally they don't sneak up on me like this," Janet said while trying to move as little as possible. "I was planning to back away when I saw the bee and to whistle from a safe distance. But I just couldn't resist these pretty flowers. I bent down to smell one and felt a tickle. And then when I stood up again it was right on my nose. Please hurry and do something! I'm afraid it's going to sting."

"Is it true that bees can smell fear?" asked Sammy. "I've always heard that."

"That's actually a very interesting scientific question," Sam replied. "While actually 'smelling fear' is, of course, impossible, there *have* been

studies suggesting that the hive defense phero-
mone secreted by bees can tag a subject with a
marker suggesting that—"

"Hush!" Mikaleh said to Sam. "You're not
helping."

Mikaleh crept closer to Janet and carefully
extended a flower she had picked.

"Here you go, friendly bee," Mikaleh said in a
soothing voice. "Don't sting my constructor. Hop
onto this yummy flower instead. It's much nicer."

The bee rubbed its front legs together, as if
considering it.

"Here little bee," Mikaleh said. "You can jump
right onto this flower. I'm sure you can. Don't
you want to show me what a big, strong bee you
are?"

The bee continued to hesitate. In the meantime, Mikaleh noticed that a large ball of nervous sweat had gathered in the folds of Janet's
forehead, just between her eyes. As the seconds
passed, it began to grow larger. Soon it would
free itself and go cascading right down the front
of her face, where it was very likely to startle the
bee.

The expression on Janet's face said that she
was well aware of this. She tried to furrow her
brow in an attempt to keep the sweat at bay.

"Hurry up, hurry up," she whispered to
Mikaleh. "The more I worry about it, the more
I'm liable to sweat!"

"Hang on just a second," Mikaleh said. "I
think he's just about to jump."

Janet's eyes crossed as she made an attempt
to look up at the bee. She began to wobble on her
feet. Mikaleh worried that she might faint.

Then it happened.

The bee began to flap its wings. Moments later, it finally took off from the end of Janet's nose. All members of the squad breathed a sigh of relief.

"Oh, thank goodness," Janet said.

"That would have been something," Sam said to nobody in particular. "She wins hundreds of battles against every kind of monster there is, but is undone in the end by a tiny bee."

The bee hovered in the air for a moment. Janet began to back away. The bee drew close to Mikaleh. As it did, she suddenly put the flower behind her back and let it fall from her hand.

"What are you doing?" Sam asked.

"I don't want to make friends with the bee," Mikaleh said. "I want him to show us where the beehives went."

"What?" Sam said.

"I have a plan," Mikaleh said. "Just trust me."

"Okay," Sam said. "Usually your plans are good. They've always worked so far. Maybe they'll also work with a bee!"

As they watched, the bee seemed to nose around Mikaleh, as if still looking for the flower. Then it abruptly shot up into the sky and took off.

Mikaleh immediately started sprinting after it. "Come on, guys," she shouted. "Don't lose sight of it!"

They all followed the bee as it flew down the hill and began to cruise off across the landscape. Mikaleh ran as fast as she could. The bee was quick, but she was just able to keep up. The squad sprinted after her.

The bee cruised across the grasslands, darting this way and that. It seemed to have lost its interest in flowers. It passed several tempting clusters of them without stopping, and instead cruised a course straight north.

"Why are we chasing this bee like this?" Sammy asked as they ran.

Perhaps because of his ninja skills, Sammy had the easiest time keeping up with the bee. He made use of his double jumps whenever the bee darted high into the sky, and always managed to keep it in sight.

"I forget who told me this," Mikaleh said. "But I've heard that when bees from beehives get separated after a fight, they always make their way back to the original beehive. There's a sort of mystical connection between them. No matter how far away they are, the bee always finds its way back. The bee is sort of a part of the beehive."

"But what if the beehive goes down in battle?" Sammy asked. "I've sliced up a number of bee-hives in my time, and I don't remember any of them leaving bees behind."

"When a beehive dies and disappears, then its bees disappear too," Mikaleh said. "They go . . . wherever husks go when they evaporate. But this bee hasn't disappeared yet."

"Which means that the beehive it's connected to is also still alive!" Sammy said.

It began to sink in. The presence of this bee indicated that at least one of the beehives—but possibly more—had made it out of the grotto after doing battle with Grumpy Joe. Which meant that they were likely to know the fate of the key, or else to have it themselves.

Mikaleh and her squad continued to follow the bee for the better part of an hour. Beehives, being essentially enhanced husks with hives of buzzing bees on their heads, did not walk particularly quickly. Certainly, they did not move more quickly than a squad of sprinting humans. Unfortunately, it was clear that the bee itself was in no particular hurry to be reunited with its master. It did tend to head generally in a northeasterly direction, but it made many false starts and wrong turns. It spent a lot of extra energy swooping high and low, and doing dramatic loops in the air.

"At least the bee is having fun," Sammy said.

"Yes," observed Sam, jogging right behind him. "It must be rare for a bee to be outside of its beehive for this long. I think it's really enjoying the personal freedom."

"Just make sure you don't lose sight of it while it's doing one of its loops," Mikaleh cautioned. "If we do, we're back to square one."

"Okay," said Sammy, leaping through the air but keeping his eye on the bee.

"Okay," said Sam.

". . . okay . . ." said a voice far in the distance behind them.

All three looked back to see Janet taking up the rear.

"Why are you so far back?" Sammy asked as he careened through the sky during a particularly extravagant jumping sequence.

". . . if the bee gets past the rest of you, I'll be like an extra measure of security back here. But for the meantime, all of you should stay up there. With the bee . . ."

They continued to race across the grassland after the bee. There were moments where Mikaleh lost it in the sun, but she always was able to find it once more. As the sun began to move lower in the sky, the group started to run out of energy. (The bee, on the other hand, seemed to have endless reserves.)

"I don't know how much longer I can run," Sam said. "Do we even know if this bee is going the right way? What if it's just gone crazy."

"It's taking us exactly where we need to go," Mikaleh said, also huffing and puffing from the long run.

"Huh?" said Sam. "How can you be sure?"

"Look down," Mikaleh said.

Sam did as she suggested. There, trampled into the grass, were the footprints of beehives. The grass did not hold prints for long, so it was obvious that whoever had made them had passed through recently. Even though the bee often whizzed from side to side, and frequently seemed to be distracted, it more or less adhered to the course that the footprints were also taking.

"That's crazy," Sam said. "Those must be the prints left by the beehives."

"Exactly," said Mikaleh.

They continued to follow both the bee and the tracks in the grass. Before long, Mikaleh began to sense something ominous in the distance. A change in the weather. A sense that the atmosphere was carrying rain. The intimation of lightning and darkness.

Namely, the coming of the Storm.

On the horizon ahead, the Storm wall came into view. Husks and mist monsters of all varieties could—of course—pass into and out of the Storm at will. Humans, on the other hand, took extreme damage when they entered the Storm. Staying inside of it for very long could be absolutely fatal.

As she chased the bee, Mikaleh nervously scanned the landscape between her position and that of the Storm wall. There were a few shrubs and trees, and a few spots where the land jutted up to make cliffs and outcroppings, but not many places where a beehive could be hiding. Mikaleh was suddenly concerned that they might be too late, and the beehive in question might have already passed into the Storm where her squad would not be able to go.

Just as this dark possibility seemed all but certain, and Mikaleh was on the point of telling the rest of her squad that catching up to their target might not happen, Mikaleh saw movement on the horizon. It was a small group of humanoid figures—four of them. They were far in the distance. They shuffled slowly in the direction of the shield wall. Their heads were distended and enormous (because, of course, their heads were covered with giant hives filled with bees).

The bee Mikaleh was chasing seemed to sense their presence, too, and began to buzz more excitedly.

"There!" Mikaleh called, gesturing to the beehives. "That's our target. Don't let them get away."

The squad bounded after the beehives. It was not clear to Mikaleh if the beehives had noticed her squad or not. Beehives were not much for sprinting or taking evasive action. As Mikaleh looked on, they continued in a slow steady shuffle in the direction of the Storm wall.

Mikaleh's team drew closer. Sam drew an automatic shotgun from his inventory and prepared to fire.

"Don't shoot yet," Mikaleh said. "Maybe it won't come to that."

"Yeah," said Sam. "But maybe it will."

They moved into a wide field and began to close the distance between themselves and the beehives. There were no natural obstacles remaining to separate them.

Suddenly, three of the four beehives stopped their retreat. They turned around and faced the squad. It was clear they meant to attack. A moment later, they began throwing bees.

"It's come to that!" Sam announced.

"It certainly has," agreed Mikaleh.

All four squad members had the same idea at precisely the same time. The long, empty expanse—combined with the considerable distance between themselves and the beehives—made the decision an easy one. All four of them immediately drew sniper rifles. Even Janet and Sammy, who usually favored hand-to-hand weapons, pulled the long scoped weapons out of their inventories and began to line up a shot.

The beehives began releasing waves of bees in their immediate area, probably with the goal of obscuring their position.

"Too little, too late," Mikaleh said aloud as she pulled the trigger on her weapon.

The sniper rifle jumped violently, and one of the beehives immediately lost its hive. The husk underneath looked alarmed and unhappy. Mikaleh reloaded and fired again, sending the creature twisting backward. It fell to the ground where it slowly disintegrated.

Mikaleh's squad members were soon firing shots of their own. A few moments later, a clattering of bullets took out the two remaining beehives. They fell on top of each other in the field and began evaporating. The wall of bees they had cast likewise began to clear.

Soon, no bees were left at all. Except, Mikaleh realized, the bee they had been chasing all this time.

Mikaleh looked again to the darkening purple horizon. There, the lone beehive that had not turned to fight continued making for the Storm. So did the bee.

The squad sprinted forward. Reaching the spot where the trio of beehives had been shot, they made a hasty inspection of the grass.

"Nothing here," Sam pronounced. "A couple of rags and honeycomb scraps. No sign of a key."

The squad nodded in agreement with this diagnosis, and again their eyes fell on the remaining beehive—now very close to the Storm wall indeed.

"Sammy, you're fastest," Mikaleh said. "Think you can catch him on foot?"

"Be a challenge, but it's worth a shot," he said.

"Then go!" Mikaleh barked, and Sammy took off across the grassland as fast as his legs would carry him. He ran like the wind, but it was hard for Mikaleh to feel optimistic. The remaining beehive had quite a head start.

Mikaleh turned to Sam and Janet. "Let's see if we can slow it down," she said, indicating their sniper rifles with a nod. "Maybe take out a leg."

"I . . ." Janet said hesitantly. "I gotta be honest. I don't trust myself at this distance. I'm just as liable to hit Sammy as the beehive."

"Yes," said Sam. "The unknowability of the crosswinds and light refractions makes the chances of such a shot very risky indeed."

"Oh," said Mikaleh, raising her sniper rifle. "Then it's a good thing I'm here to take some risks."

Mikaleh looked down her scope and adjusted the range. The beehive was now hundreds of yards away. This would be the longest shot she had ever taken in a real combat situation. She wanted to avoid killing the beehive if possible. Ideally, she could take out a knee or a foot and give Sammy time to catch up.

She risked lowering the weapon again and watched Sammy racing through the grass toward the beehive. He was moving quite quickly. The beehive was near the Storm wall, but there was still a chance he might catch it.

Then Sammy suddenly disappeared.

Mikaleh was looking at Sammy, then she looked back to the slowly retreating beehive, then back to where Sammy had been. And nothing was there.

An instant of complete confusion followed.

On the wind Mikaleh heard Sammy's voice: "Ow! I've twisted my ankle. Are these gopher holes? Who put these here?"

Using her sniper scope, Mikaleh found Sammy. He was curled on the ground and inspecting his rapidly purpling ankle. She winced in sympathy for her squadmate—ankle sprains were unpleasant for anybody—but soon remembered what this meant. There was no chance of him catching up to the beehive. A well-placed shot from her sniper rifle was now their only hope.

"Hurry," Janet said from behind Mikaleh. "It's almost to the Storm wall."

"I'm sure Mikaleh can see that," said Sam. "You can see that, can't you Mikaleh? So you should probably take a shot now. Because it's our only hope."

Mikaleh tried to ignore the well-meaning voices of her squad and focus only on the retreating beehive. It was now perhaps five steps from entering the Storm wall. Mikaleh held her breath, tried to keep the creature in her crosshairs, and counted its steps in her head.

5 . . .

4 . . .

"Ahh . . ."

2 . . .

"CHOO!"

As Mikaleh pulled the trigger on her sniper rifle, Janet let out possibly the biggest sneeze that Mikaleh had ever heard.

It frightened nearby wildlife. Birds flying in the sky overhead stopped and looked. And, most assuredly, it startled Mikaleh enough to make her shot go wide.

Minutes later, Mikaleh watched helplessly as the beehive passed into the Storm and out of sight. Mikaleh lowered her weapon, turned around, and put her hand on her hip.

"What?" said Janet. "I'm very allergic to pollen, and these grasslands are full of it."

"You couldn't have held it in for another second?" Sam asked.

"Believe me, I was trying to," Janet said.

Mikaleh just shook her head. "C'mon," she told her squad. "Let's go see if Sammy's leg is okay."

It was. The squad jogged over and found that Sammy was already righting himself in the grass. He steadied himself, using his sword like a cane, and tested his hurt ankle gingerly.

"Careful guys," he said as the rest of the squad drew close. "There really are gopher holes all over the place. Somebody should put up a sign or something. Or maybe just scare away the gophers."

"Are you okay?" Mikaleh asked.

"I think so," Sammy said. "I can usually recover pretty quickly from something like this. Sorry I didn't catch up to the beehive. I really thought I'd be able to get it."

"Don't worry," Mikaleh said. "I know you did your best."

Sam sat down on the grass. He lay back, put his hands behind his head, and closed his eyes.

"What are *you* doing?" Sammy said.

"Resting," Sam said. "Trying to think of our next move. But mostly resting."

"We can't just give up," Sammy said.

"Logically, I don't see what we can do now," Sam said. "That beehive has probably made his way quite deep into the Storm at this point. If you want to run in and be destroyed, be my guest. Personally, I'm trying to think of another trail we can pick up for finding the key. I think this one has just gone cold. Plus, like I said, I'm also resting from all the running we just did chasing that bee!"

Mikaleh—who had been silently considering their next move—suddenly sprang to life.

"That's it!" she said.

"Huh?" said Sam, opening his eyes again. "What's *it*?"

"The bee," Mikaleh said. "*It* hasn't passed into the Storm wall yet. It can't have. It was just here. Help me look."

All four squad members searched the sky for the tiny bee.

"Got it," announced Janet. "It's over there, headed for the Storm wall."

Mikaleh squinted in the direction where Janet was frantically gesturing. Then she saw it too. Headed for the edge of the Storm wall, at the very same place where the beehive had entered, was a fat, lazy bumblebee.

"Good job, Janet," Mikaleh said. "You stay here on account of your allergies. You two, come with me."

Mikaleh took off at a tear, racing after the bee. Sam and Sammy did their best to keep up. (True to his forecasting, Sammy's injured leg proved surprisingly resilient.)

"I don't understand," Sam said as he ran. "Why are we still trying to catch the bee?"

"Just trust me" was all Mikaleh said.

They ran as fast as their legs would carry them, and, this time, they *were* in time.

They arrived at the gently curving border of the Storm wall just as the bee did. Mikaleh reached out and caught the bee between her gloved hands.

"Quick!" she said. "One of you craft an enclosure around me. Give it a roof and a door, but no windows."

"What?" said Sam. "Why? Also, what material should I use? Stone is increasingly trendy these days, but wood has always—"

"*Just build it!*" Mikaleh shouted. "Now! Before I get stung!"

Sam and Sammy both shrugged but began to build a simple enclosure as quickly as they could. Mikaleh clearly seemed to feel that speed was of the essence, so they used wood, the material that was always quickest to craft with. In mere moments, a tiny hut had sprung up around her. When the roof was finished and they were sealed off from the sky, Mikaleh immediately released the bee from her hands.

The bee did not move to sting her, but hovered in the air by her face for a moment as if to ask: "What was *that* about?" Its tiny compound eyes probed her face for an explanation. Then it turned its attention back to entering the Storm wall . . . which was now impossible, because it was inside the enclosure.

The bee immediately registered frustration. It probed the edges of the little hut, looking for a way out. Then, after it found none, it began to bang itself slowly against the wall nearest to the Storm, as if to say "Hey, let me out, will ya?"

Meanwhile, Mikaleh backed carefully away and let herself out through the hut's lone door. She quickly closed it behind her.

Sammy and Sam looked at each other, then at Mikaleh.

"So . . . we just caught a bee?" Sam asked.

Mikaleh nodded.

"Why?" said Sammy. "It doesn't have a gold key with a ruby handle. I don't think a bee could even carry a key. It would be bigger and heavier than the bee was."

"But wait," said Sam. "Aren't bees supposed to be able to carry fifty times their own body weight? No, sorry. I'm thinking of ants. But maybe a bee could still do it. How heavy is gold? Also, are we talking pure gold, or just gold-plated?"

"I have trouble thinking Droopy would make all this trouble over a gold-*plated* key," Sammy said. "I'm thinking it's the real thing, through and through."

"Quiet, you two!" Mikaleh said.

Sam and Sammy looked a little hurt, but clammed up.

"Sorry, that was a bit . . . abrupt," Mikaleh quickly added. "You know I love you guys, but sometimes you have a way of getting a little unfocused."

"My bad," said Sam. "But what *should* we be focused on, if not bees carrying keys?"

"Yeah," said Sammy. "I still don't get the point of what we just did."

Mikaleh decided she had better explain herself.

"This is just a theory," she began. "But all theories have to be tested sometime. We know that bees and beehives are connected, and whenever a bee is loosed, it eventually tries to return to its hive. So—mostly because I was out of other ideas—I thought we should see if that connection works both ways."

"Both ways?" Sam asked.

"Maybe the bee misses the beehive where it used to live, but also . . . maybe the beehive misses the bee."

Sam and Sammy looked at each other again.

"So you're saying the beehive might . . . *come back* for the bee?" Sam asked.

"I'd probably do that if I was a beehive," Sammy said after considering it. "The bees are practically a part of the beehive. If I lost a part of me—like a tooth or something—I'd definitely come back and find it again."

"That's weird," said Sam.

"No, it's not," Sammy countered. "I don't want somebody else picking up my teeth."

"Why?" said Sam. "You're not using them anymore."

"But they could totally claim my tooth fairy money. And that's not fair. That money is rightfully mine!"

While the twins (probably) fought about teeth, Mikaleh turned and signaled to Janet that it was now safe for her to approach. Janet cautiously made her way over to the little hut.

"Don't worry," said Mikaleh. "The bee is trapped inside."

"I can hear it buzzing," Janet said. "It's loud and angry."

"Yeah," Mikaleh agreed. "And I hope that beehive can hear it too."

For several minutes they waited. The bee—which seemed to have boundless energy—continued flapping its wings in frustration and banging itself against the wall of the hut. Mikaleh looked deep into the Storm wall, but saw nothing. Seeing inside the Storm was something of an art in and of itself. The Storm was like a strange purple lens. Things passing beyond the Storm wall were always distorted out of proportion, but they did not always become invisible, at least not immediately. Sometimes if you squinted just right, you could make an educated guess about what might lurk on the other side. Mikaleh's guesses weren't right all of the time, but she was at least batting .500.

She sat on the roof of the hut that held the bee and looked into the Storm. She had not had to do this in some time, and the proximity once again drove home the utter strangeness of it. What was the Storm? Nobody knew for sure. Was it a gateway to another dimension? Was it, itself, the other dimension? Or was it something else entirely. Something beyond the power of humans to understand.

Whatever it was, Mikaleh decided it didn't have much action going on inside at the moment, at least not in the part near her squad.

Mikaleh began to think they needed to be a bit more aggressive in their approach. She hopped down from the hut and walked over to where the rest of the squad was waiting.

"Which one of you was the last to go into the Storm?" she asked them.

The squad members considered it.

"Wasn't it you, Sammy?" Janet said. "You accidentally lost your grip on one of your swords when you were fighting a lobber right on the border of the Storm the other day."

"Oh, that's right," Sammy said. "It didn't go deep into the Storm, so I just ducked in to get it. Not much of a big deal. Not that it felt good, though. I mean, I don't have to explain that to you guys."

This was true. He didn't.

The pain that a human felt when venturing into the Storm was as hard to describe as it was to experience. For Sammy, it felt like taking a topical heat rub—the kind you were supposed to use just a little of when your muscles were sore—and injecting it directly into your nerves. Other humans said it felt like electrocution, being set on fire, or being electrocuted while you were also set on fire. Others had invoked being burned by acid or poked by a thousand tiny invisible knives all at once from every direction.

Yet while it was extremely unpleasant to go into the Storm—and could be fatal within a minute or two—very short incursions were not usually life threatening. They just hurt like the dickens.

"I think our beehive might need some urging to come find his bee," Mikaleh said. "Does anybody wanna volunteer, or should I do it myself?"

The squad looked at one another and swallowed hard.

Then Janet raised her hand.

"It should be me," she said. "I'm the one who couldn't catch the bee because I was allergic to it. And then I sneezed and made Mikaleh miss her shot."

"None of those things are really your fault, properly speaking," Sam said.

"Yeah," said Sammy. "It's not like you were sniffing a bunch of pollen on purpose while Mikaleh was lining up her shot."

"Are you volunteering to go in my place?" Janet asked.

"Oh, goodness no!" Sammy said.

Janet dutifully walked up to the Storm wall.

"How should I do this?" she asked Mikaleh.

"I don't think you need to go all the way in," Mikaleh said. "Just kind of stick your head in and shout."

"I think I understand," said Janet. "I'll take it from here."

Janet took several deep breaths and closed her eyes tight.

"Oh my gosh," she said to herself. "This is going to *stink.*"

Then she stuck her head through and shouted into the Storm as loudly as she could.

"HEY, BEEHIVE! DON'T YOU WANT TO COME BACK FOR YOUR BEE? IT MISSES YOU SO BAD! IT'S YOUR FAVORITE BEE. BUZZ BUZZ! COME GET IT!"

When she could bear it no longer, Janet pulled her head back out of the Storm. Her face was flushed and she was breathing hard.

"Gah," she said. "That was like a scalp massage from Edward Scissorhands. Ouch!"

"Thanks for doing that," Mikaleh said. "That could really make the difference. Now we just have to sit back and see if it works."

The squad resumed watching the Storm wall, trying to make sense of the strange shapes and shadows that seemed to lurk just on the other side. After a few moments, some of the darker, creepier shapes seemed to crystallize and solidify into a roughly human-sized blob. It looked like a person but had a very large, cylindrical head.

"Hey, guys," Mikaleh said. "I think this might be it."

The squad took a few steps back from the Storm wall to give the shape some room. At first it hesitated there, as if making up its mind. Then it began to push through. A loud buzzing came with it.

A smiled curled Mikaleh's lips.

"Looking for something?" she asked.

Mikaleh instantly wondered if this was the right phrasing. Beehives had no clear way of seeing. The hives that covered their heads were totally opaque, and there were no holes to be seen. Mikaleh wondered if they used echolocation, like a bat.

The beehive pushed the rest of the way through. It did not answer Mikaleh, but neither did it start throwing bees around, which Mikaleh decided to count as a win.

The beehive cocked its head to the side as if listening.

"Your little friend is over here, inside this hut," Mikaleh said.

The beehive cautiously took a step nearer.

"You can talk to us," Mikaleh urged. "We spoke to a husk last night. We know you can talk. At this point, we're practically husk whisperers."

The beehive took a few tentative steps. It seemed to examine the wall of the hut but did not break it down as husks usually did. Then it looked over at Mikaleh.

A sound like vocal chords being vibrated by a hundred buzzing bees came from it.

"Can talk. Yes. Choose to talk? Why? Where is my bee?"

"Your bee is safe and will be back with you in just a moment," Mikaleh said. "First we need to ask you a few questions."

"Why?" buzzed the beehive. "Why should I help a bunch of humans who just shot up all of my friends?"

"In our defense, they were throwing bees at us," Sam pointed out.

Mikaleh gave him a look that said this was not important at the moment.

"You should help us because we know about the gold key with the red ruby handle . . . and we know about the Last Survivor."

To say that the exterior of a beehive could, in any meaningful way, become expressive was not something Mikaleh would have thought possible. But she had to believe her own eyes. As she looked on, the exterior of the hive seemed to lose its will to hold up. The sides slackened. The very architecture of the thing seemed to dissemble for a moment. Even the bees themselves living in the hive seemed to droop. Their buzzing became lazy and sad.

"You do?" the talking hive said.

"We do?" Janet said from a few paces off. "Because I thought the Last Survivor was just something a crazy old man liked to talk about. And the specifics on the key are still more than a little in question. We don't even know what it looked like. Also—"

"Shhhhh!" the rest of the squad said in unison.

"Oh, right," said Janet. "Sorry."

It was not immediately clear if the beehive had been following what Janet said.

"Look . . ." the beehive said. "I . . . uh . . . I think we should talk."

Several moments later, the beehive took a seat near the hut. Mikaleh, Sam, and Sammy sat near it, cross-legged on the grass.

"Please begin whenever you're ready," Mikaleh said, hoping to prompt the beehive to speak.

"Okay," it said with a buzz. "But why is that one woman sitting so far away?"

"That's Janet," Mikaleh said. "She's allergic to bees. It's nothing personal."

"But why have you put tape over her mouth like that?" the beehive pressed.

"It's, uh, a game we play," Mikaleh said. "Like a contest. To see how long you can sit quietly with tape over your mouth. Trust me. We humans find it lots of fun."

"Your people are truly quite strange," the beehive said.

"Now, what did you have to tell us?" Mikaleh asked.

The beehive seemed to shift thoughtfully and hesitantly, as though it wished to be very careful about what it would say next.

"I think that we should share what we know," it said. "We should *both* share."

"Fine," Mikaleh said. "But you go first. Age before beauty, as the saying goes. Though in your case maybe it should just be 'head full of bees before head not full of bees.'"

The beehive shifted in its seat as if unsure what this meant.

"I think you're confusing it, Mikaleh," Sam said.

"Hey, this is my first time talking to a beehive," she said. "And my second time talking to a husk *ever*. If you think you could do a better job, please be my guest."

Then, even as it hesitated, something in the beehive seemed to change. It began speaking.

"I should not be talking to you humans, but no other husks are around to see me do it. And things must be desperate indeed if *humans* know about the Last Survivor."

The beehive said the h-word ("humans") as if the term was quite distasteful.

"We know something about it," Mikaleh said, even if this was something of a stretch. Mikaleh knew that it was bad to stretch the truth, and only did so in extreme circumstances. She considered sitting down to chat with a beehive to be among them. It would be a challenge to get the beehive to tell what it knew about the Last Survivor, without having much knowledge of her own to share in return. However, Mikaleh thought she might be able to do it if she proceeded carefully. (She also reflected that putting tape over Janet's mouth had definitely been a good idea.)

"Tell me the story of how you have come to know of the Last Survivor," the beehive said.

"I mean, we've known about it for a while," Mikaleh said.

"Why do you say 'it'?" the beehive wondered. "There is no need to be rude. I mean, everybody gets to choose their pronouns, I guess. But I never heard that the Last Survivor wanted to be called 'it.'"

Mikaleh realized that she had perhaps already made a misstep.

"So the Last Survivor is a person, not a thing," Sam whispered.

"Shh," Mikaleh whispered back. "Act like we already knew that."

The beehive looked back and forth between Sam and Mikaleh, obviously still wondering if they could be trusted.

"Go on," the beehive said.

"Well, our latest encounter with the Last Survivor—who is definitely a person, and not a thing—came when we got an invitation from a certain husk with a particularly droopy neck," Mikaleh said.

"You have seen him!" the beehive said, suddenly very excited. "Where?"

"I'll tell you that," Mikaleh said carefully. "But first you should take a turn sharing some of the things that you know. For example, why were you and the other beehives in that grotto fighting with Grumpy Joe. I'm guessing it wasn't just because he was grumpy."

"Actually, for a mist monster he wasn't that grumpy at all," the beehive said. "That name was sort of ironic. Like how you might call a big person 'Tiny.' But anyhow, why do you *think* we were there?"

"The gold key with the ruby handle," Mikaleh said.

"That's right," said the buzzing hive. "We got word that Grumpy Joe had it. We went to ask him if he did. You'd think he would have been cooperative about something so important, but husks and mist monsters are not always friendly with one another—contrary to what humans might think. Some things were said. Some accusations were made. One thing led to another, and a fight broke out."

"And that was the end of Grumpy Joe," said Sammy.

"And the end of quite a few beehives, too," said the beehive. "There were twenty of us when we went into that grotto. Only four came out. And now there is only me."

"Did Grumpy Joe have the key?" Mikaleh asked.

The beehive buzzed to indicate annoyance.

"Would I be sitting here talking to you if he had it? No, of course he didn't. We searched the entire grotto. There was nothing to be found. Even a small grotto takes hours to search. It was quite a task."

"We know that," Sam said. "We were just there, and we did the same thing."

"So now I have told you something," said the beehive. "Now *you* will tell *me* something. Where did you see that husk? 'Droopy' is indeed the right word for him. I shall have to remember that. His appearance is quite odd."

Mikaleh thought it was a stretch for anybody wearing a beehive on their head to be criticizing the appearance of other people. But considering the situation, she decided to let it slide.

"We might have run into him in Stonewood," Mikaleh said carefully. "And he also thought that Grumpy Joe might have the key. We agreed to go and have a look. But obviously, your team had beat us to it."

"I always knew he was driven by something irrational," the beehive said. "If he is enlisting squads of humans to help him, then he has transcended even irrationality. This is madness. Clearly he must be stopped."

"So . . ." Mikaleh said carefully. "Why do you guys want the gold key with the ruby handle?"

"That should be obvious," said the beehive. "To prevent anyone from releasing the Last Survivor. But you would not have asked that question if you truly understood. I am beginning to think that maybe your squad has stumbled into something *beyond* your understanding. If this is the case, I advise you to consider going home and forgetting about all of this. The husks—and, yes, perhaps the mist monsters—will settle this among ourselves. It is better for humans not to interfere."

The beehive stood as though it would now depart. It took a few steps toward the wall of the Storm, then stopped.

"I almost forgot," it said. "May I please have my bee now?"

Sam and Sammy looked at Mikaleh. She gave a nod. Sam opened the door to the hut and released the bee. It quickly exited the hut and headed directly into the hive. Soon, it was lost among a hundred others just like it.

"Thank you," the beehive said. "Remember my words. Stay out of this if you know what's good for you."

And with that, it disappeared back into the Storm. The Storm wall made a flash of white and purple as the beehive passed through, and then it was gone entirely.

"What was that about?" Sam asked.

"Yeah, I'm still not clear about why the beehives care about the Last Survivor . . . but it's clear that they *do* care," said Sammy.

"Mmmmm mmm mmmm?" mumbled Janet.

"Someone help Janet with her tape," Mikaleh said.

Sammy peeled the tape from around Janet's mouth.

"Ow," she said. "But thank you."

"What were you asking?" Mikaleh said.

"I was asking how the beehives know about Droopy," Janet said. "Because it's clear that they do. This is all connected in some strange way."

"I agree with you," Mikaleh said. "We've just got to figure out what it is."

The squad stared doubtfully into the Storm wall.

"What do we do now?" asked Janet. "I feel like we're at a dead end. I was hoping we would learn something new from the beehive, but we didn't learn anything at all. Not anything that tells us where to find the key, at any rate."

"I think you may be mistaken," Mikaleh said. "I think we learned something very important today. Namely, that the Last Survivor exists and the husks know about him . . . or her. This might not tell us where to find the key. But I think it tells us what our next steps should be."

"What's that?" asked Janet.

Mikaleh's response was firm and assured.

"We're going to find the Traveler."

CHAPTER FIVE

The squad trekked through a thick forest on the outskirts of a suburb filled with modest homes and an abandoned strip mall built in the times before the Storm. The woods were filled with light and animals. The sun shone brightly through the trees.

"The last place I saw him was at a settlement just up ahead," Mikaleh said. "I think this is as good a place to start as any."

"I feel so bad for not taking him seriously back in the day," said Janet. "When he was around, I just thought he was a crazy man. I thought the things he said were just nonsense. Now it's like learning that the nonsense words the crazy man was saying were actually the names of all the stocks I needed to buy to become a millionaire."

"How could you have known?" asked Sam.

"I don't think I could have," said Janet. "None of us could have. But now we do. So let's go be millionaires! . . . in a manner of speaking."

As they approached the suburb where other groups of survivors had constructed a settlement of forts and shields, Mikaleh privately hoped that she was doing the right thing. The more she thought about the Last Survivor, the more anxious she became. It had gone from the ravings of a hobo to something that seemed to involve the entire husk community. She had the feeling of someone who has just walked into someone else's party. You don't know who is who, or what game everyone is playing, but you just try to keep cool and fit in. But also, instead of *people* at the party, it's murderous husks who just might try to attack you at any given moment. And then also you've brought along your best friends and put them in danger too . . . It was a funny feeling, and not entirely pleasant. Mikaleh did her best to keep a brave face and make it look like she felt confident and knew what she was doing. Sometimes, in a zombie apocalypse filled with husks and monsters, *looking* brave was the next best thing to actually being brave. And sometimes looking brave was the best you were going to get.

They exited the forest and began to approach the settlement-proper. Surviving humans had used one of the old strip malls as a starting point to build a base filled with the kind of amenities survivors might need. It had a workshop, a gun range, and then a second gun range in case the first one broke. It was like a small city, filled with the hustle and bustle of people at work.

The squad began heading for the large front door of the settlement—twelve feet tall and reinforced against husk attacks—but Mikaleh steered them around the side of the perimeter instead.

"Wait, where are we going?" asked Sam. "I thought you said this was the last place you saw the Traveler."

"It was," Mikaleh said. "But he wouldn't be inside with all the skilled, hardworking people who are—you know—actually earning their keep."

"He wouldn't?" said Sam.

"No," Mikaleh said. "I think we want to look around here, near the rear of the encampment."

Sam was not sure he understood, but Mikaleh seemed so brave and confident that he decided to trust her.

Sure enough, camped at the back of the settlement—in an undefended position where the strip mall abutted the forest—were several scruffy-looking people in crude tents. They looked like they were not doing very much of anything, as though their only goal was to avoid working hard. Most of them were relaxing on the ground.

"I wonder what these kind of people used to be," Janet said as Mikaleh looked them over. "You know, *before* the Storm."

"I think we can make some educated guesses," Mikaleh responded. "Con artists. Grifters. People who would go to great lengths to steal subway tokens out of vending machines. You know, that sort."

As Mikaleh made this appraisal, one scruffy man wearing a very old and tattered tuxedo took notice of the squad. He hopped to his feet, spit on his hand and slicked down his hair, and grinned a bright grin that showed several missing teeth. Then he sauntered over confidently.

"Hello, strangers," he said like a used car salesman. "I can tell from your being armed to the teeth and whatnot that you are a group deeply concerned with staying safe from husks."

"Actually, they tend to be more concerned with staying safe from *us*," Mikaleh said, only half paying attention to the scruffy man. She scanned the rest of the stragglers, looking for the Traveler.

"Well, whatever your situation, you'll want to be sure you have some of my world-famous husk repellent in your inventory," the shabby man said. "Made from the most exotic herbs and balms. A mystical recipe as old as the Storm itself. Which is not that old, but still."

"Uh-huh," Mikaleh said doubtfully.

"In fact," the pitchman continued, "I'm wearing some right now. And look. Not a husk in sight. Who could argue with those results?"

"Look, we're not interested in any husk repellent right now," Mikaleh said. "We're actually looking for a person. I used to see him around here in the early days, right after the Storm hit. He was old and he used to wear a long gray overcoat, and people called him the Traveler. He told stories. Do you know anybody like that?"

"Well, sure I know him," the shabby man said. "I . . . I just have to remember where. It's such a challenge to jog my memory these days. Something in the Storm has made me more forgetful than I used to be. If only I had something that would assist me. Some supplies or weapons, for example, might help me to think. Or one of those cool katana swords your friend has. That would *really* aid my memory."

Sammy's face showed that he was horrified by this notion. He took a couple of steps backward.

"Wait," said Janet. "How is a ninja sword going to help you thi— Ooooh! You want a bribe. Now I've got it."

"Let's call it a 'donation,'" the man said. "Seems more tasteful that way. I find couching things in the right words can go a long way toward making folks receptive. Like giving me a bribe. Which you should do right now."

Suddenly, a high—almost squeaky—voice said: "Don't you listen to him!"

Mikaleh looked up. A much-younger tramp was approaching. He couldn't have been more than nine or ten years old, yet he had the world-weary manner of a much-older person. Mikaleh always felt sorry for youngsters, because they had so little memory of life before the Storm. But this youngster didn't seem to be spending any time feeling sorry for himself. He brushed past the scruffy man as though he were there to take charge.

"Don't listen to this one," the boy said. "He knows where the Traveler is just as sure as that bottle of old skin lotion he found is going to keep husks away. Which is not at all."

The scruffy man appeared defensive.

"If my lotion—I mean, husk repellent—doesn't work, then why're there no husks around?"

The boy replied skeptically: "If it *does* work, then why are you always the first to run sprinting inside the barricades when the husks *do* attack."

"You can never be too careful," the scruffy man replied brightly, with the verbal dexterity of a true confidence man.

"Seriously, don't listen to him," the boy said to Mikaleh. "The Traveler *was* here. I know the one you mean. But he's not around now."

"Shhh," said the scruffy man. "You're going to fudge the deal."

The boy seemed to ignore this, and kept talking.

"The Traveler left a while ago. He was always coming and going. But a few weeks ago, we heard he was headed for the survivor settlement in North Canny Valley."

Mikaleh had heard of this settlement. It was a dangerous outpost. It had no neighbors, a faulty shield system, and was constantly being overrun by hordes of slavering husks. It was not a place to go if longevity was your goal.

"Why would he go *there*?" Mikaleh asked.

"Why does that guy do anything?" said the youngster. "He's as confusing as he is crazy. But there are times when he's not so crazy. Like he'll say things that seem totally nuts—like they make no sense at all—but then they turn out to be true."

"That sounds like you actually *do* know him," Mikaleh said. "I'm inclined to believe you. Thanks. Here, I think that you deserve a reward."

Mikaleh reached into her inventory and pulled out a jug of Slurp Juice with a large cork stopper in the top.

"Wow!" said the boy, happily accepting it.

"Use it whenever you get in a jam," Mikaleh said.

Then she turned to the scruffy man. "As for you, you can have an apple."

The man cocked his head to the side and stuck out his lower lip thoughtfully. His expression said that an apple wasn't so bad for a few minutes of grifting.

"But it comes with the condition that I want you to stop trying to cheat people, and earn an honest living instead," Mikaleh added, holding out the shiny red fruit.

"Thanks, but no thanks," the scruffy man said with a rueful smile. "No apple is worth that."

"Suit yourself," Mikaleh said.

She put the apple back into her inventory. The man in the dirty tuxedo walked back to the other hobos at the back of the strip mall, and sat down on the grass.

"North Canny Valley Outpost, eh?" Mikaleh said. "That's a pretty grim place, but if that's where we've got to go, then so be it."

"I actually think Canny Valley is beautiful this time of year," said Janet. "The Storm has pretty well messed up the seasons, so really, it's beautiful all the time now. But that's not a bad way for things to be. If you can ignore the sudden and vigorous husk attacks, it's a very pretty place."

"I just wonder what the Traveler is doing there," Mikaleh said.

"Yeah," offered Sammy. "I can think of more dangerous outposts, but there aren't many."

Then Mikaleh said: "If life has taught me anything—especially life during the Storm—it's that sometimes you have to have a little bit of trust to get by. I'm going to trust that the Traveler has a reason for doing what he does. For the moment, we've got to let that be enough."

Mikaleh turned back to the boy, who was peering excitedly through the glass sides of the jug of Slurp Juice.

"Did the Traveler say anything about what route he was taking? Was he making other stops, or was he going straight to North Canny Valley?"

"Straight there was how I heard it," said the boy. "But with the Traveler, you never really know, do you?"

"That's absolutely right," Mikaleh said. "You don't."

CHAPTER SIX

The sun shone down hard in Canny Valley, because it always did. Mikaleh struggled to think of any other place where it was more reliably hot, dry, and sunny. Maybe, in the time before the Storm, Sedona, Arizona, had been something like it. Mikaleh could remember traveling there with her parents on vacation as a little girl. It was possible that Canny Valley actually *was* Sedona, Mikaleh reasoned. When the Storm had come, the network of places left untouched had become changed and hard to identify. Different locales had been smooshed together. Now and then you might see a leftover signpost showing the name of a town, but so many towns had the same name. Which had been which? The electronics that humans had grown so accustomed to using to track their movements had all ceased to function normally. Physical maps, when you could still find them, were all wrong now.

Sometimes Mikaleh wondered how exactly the Storm had moved parts of the maps closer together. Was their new "known world" a sort of

Pangea combining different lands and places in some entirely new way?

It often felt like it.

As Mikaleh led her squad into Canny Valley, she was unable to tell if the mesas and rock formations were the same ones she might have seen so many years ago in Arizona, or if they were something entirely new.

They prepared to enter a crevasse that would take them between two impressive rock formations. Suddenly, Janet piped up.

"Do you think you would still recognize the Traveler? I'm not sure I would."

"I mean, I *think* so," said Mikaleh. "I didn't used to pay that much attention to him. But he was sort of oddly distinctive."

"That's a good way of putting it," Janet agreed. "Quite distinctive indeed."

It was near to noon—not quite the hottest part of the day in Canny Valley, but close to it. The squad kept their eyes on the sky, hoping some of the intermittent cloud cover might chance to settle above them for a while. It was very dry and very warm.

During one of these hopeful surveys of the near horizon, Sammy began pointing.

"Hey," he said. "Do you guys see that? There's like a . . . flashing way at the top of that rock formation over there."

The squad stopped and looked. Mikaleh would not have called it a "flashing" exactly, but something at the top of a rocky hill certainly glinted and glimmered when it caught the noonday sun. In another situation, Mikaleh might have been concerned that it could be the sun's rays catching the scope of a sniper rifle. There were no survivors in the immediate area, however. And the shimmering wasn't quite right for a sniper's scope.

"Could it be someone signaling to us?" Mikaleh wondered aloud.

"Almost definitely not," Sam replied, as if very confident of his answer. "I know Morse code, I know semaphore signals, and I know what it looks like when you've got a piece of mirror or chrome and you're just waving it like crazy to get somebody's attention from far away. And that's not any of those. That's like something catching the sun accidentally. Maybe a crow picked up something shiny, and it's got a nest up there."

"Bro, I think the only kind of birds in Canny Valley are vultures, and they only pick up things they're going to eat," said Sammy.

Mikaleh—who still wanted to know if Sam and Sammy were actual twins or brothers or what— meditated on the possible meanings of 'bro' in that sentence. (She knew she could have once asked Sam and Sammy how—and if—they were related, but now so much time had passed that she would feel stupid for asking. She still hoped that one day they would let slip something that would make it absolutely clear.)

Janet gazed up at the strange intermittent shimmering and tried to think about it from a constructor's point of view.

"It would be strange to build something up there that glimmered so much," she opined. "You'd have to be interested in trying to attract people to it. But if that were your goal, even novice builders can craft things that are more eye-catching. So I'm kind of with the crow theory, even if there aren't any crows around here. It looks like something that somebody left up there accidentally. The only question is, do we go and investigate?"

The squad exchanged glances. It was clear to Mikaleh that they were quite curious.

"Well," said Mikaleh, "I doubt the Traveler is going to get up and leave in the next few minutes . . . wherever he is. I reckon we've got time to climb to the top of that hill. And who knows? It might end up being faster than going around."

"Yesss," said Janet. "I'm excited to see what it is."

"Sure," said Mikaleh. "Just be careful. The way up looks steep. Climbing can be just as challenging as defeating a husk. More so, even."

"I hear you," said Janet. "We've never been defeated by the toughest mist monster, so I'm going to make darn sure that we don't get defeated by a hill."

Their new course decided, the squad turned off the beaten bath and began to head up the red rock and gravel hill that lay directly before them. In the distance at the top, the strange glistening continued—twinkling almost as if the hill itself were saying hello. Mikaleh was not sure how she felt about this. She shielded her eyes and began to make the ascent.

The ground underfoot was silty and fine. Sam and Sammy, who led the pack, found that this made for slow going.

"Uh," Sammy said. "This is like playing beach volleyball. It looks so easy, but when you actually try it, jumping or just taking a step is, like, really hard."

"I know," said Sam. "I'm just hoping there aren't any sand spiders or scorpions. Those are even lousier than playing beach volleyball."

"Aww, this isn't so bad at all," Janet boomed, picking up speed and barreling past them. "I don't see a scorpion anywhere. I bet I can beat both of you to the top!"

Sammy looked at Sam.

"We better try to keep her from beating us," Sammy said. "Whenever she beats us at something, she gloats endlessly."

"Agreed," said Sam. "And that's *no* fun to be around."

With Janet barreling for the top of the hill, and Sam and Sammy trailing after, it was all Mikaleh could do to stay within shouting distance.

As she watched her squad scramble up near the top of the hill, Mikaleh got a better view of the reflective shimmering. It now took on the aspect of movement. As though something shiny and mirrorlike were being jostled around up there. Mikaleh still wondered what it could be.

Then Janet came within several feet of the top of the hill. (She had beaten Sam and Sammy by several yards, and the gloating would no doubt be epic.) Suddenly, as the reflective hilltop came into view for her, Janet froze. She quickly turned around and headed back down the hill. Her expression looked as though she had just seen an elderly relative naked.

As Janet reached Sam and Sammy, she grabbed each one of them by an ear and pulled them back in the other direction.

"Ow!" said Sammy. "What gives?"

"No fair," said Sam. "Everyone knows ear grabbing is cheating."

Janet kept going until she reached Mikaleh, and deposited the twins at the squad leader's feet.

Mikaleh inclined her head to the side, looking for an explanation.

Janet was breathing so hard that for a moment she couldn't speak. She held up a single finger, telling Mikaleh she needed a moment. In the meantime, Sam and Sammy rubbed their ears to get the circulation back.

"Chrome . . ." Janet said when she had enough breath for one word.

"Chrome huskies . . ." she said when she had enough for two.

"Oh," said Mikaleh. "Well, that makes sense. You do find them in Canny Valley from time to time. Looking back, I really should have guessed."

"So there are two or three chrome huskies up at the top of the hill?" Sammy asked. "That shouldn't be so alarming. They don't used ranged weapons, and we can always take out a group that size with long guns."

Janet was still catching her breath. "Two or three . . ." she managed.

"Yes, that's what I just said," Sammy clarified.

"Hundred . . ." Janet added.

"What?" said Sammy.

"Two or three hundred . . ." Janet said, the look of alarm never leaving her eyes.

"Hundreds of them would be an entirely different prospect," Sam said, pushing his glasses up his nose. "My studies of the chrome husky are nowhere close to my research on the husk, but hundreds of them are a problem. They have such high health in the first place, and they'll keep reviving literally forever if you don't hit them with a fire or water weapon. Hundreds of those is quite a problem indeed."

"I didn't look for long," said Janet, her powers of speech returning. "But they seemed to be massing on the other side of the hill. A giant gathering. I've never seen anything like it."

Mikaleh had to look for herself. "You guys stay here," she told them. "I'm going to take a peek."

Mikaleh crept to the top of the hill. When she came close to the peak, she fell to her stomach and began crawling forward inch by inch. (Sand in her clothes seemed a small price to pay.) She began to peer over into the far side of the hill.

There, just a few feet away, was the largest collection of chrome huskies that Mikaleh had ever seen. It was the largest collection of *any* kind of husk that she had ever seen. Two or three hundred looked like a conservative estimate. The sight of so much chrome in the open sun was nearly blinding, so it was hard to look for very long. Yet as near as Mikaleh could tell, the chrome huskies seemed to be celebrating. There was a strange convivial mood. The creatures did not look violent. They relaxed with one another, and many of them actually smiled. This was very strange behavior for any kind of husk. Mikaleh was more than a little confused. She carefully retreated down her side of the hill.

"That's one of the craziest things I've ever seen," said Mikaleh. "And I've seen some pretty crazy stuff! They're just hanging out together and socializing. They aren't being violent or anything."

"Why would hundreds of chrome huskies assemble like that?" asked Sammy. "There's not a base of humans to attack anywhere in the vicinity."

"I think that might be the point," said Sam, suddenly piping up. "Like I said before, I know regular husks better than chrome huskies, but regular husks often like to get together and relax in a situation where they don't have to be 'on.' Keep in mind that slobbering and violently attacking buildings and humans is *work* for a husk. And sometimes they just want to hang out after a long day of breaking things and chasing people around. I expect the chrome huskies are the same way. Now, your typical husk takes several breaks throughout the year, but what it really looks forward to is the annual Gathering of the Husks. Very few humans have observed this and lived to tell about it, but there have been enough sightings that I believe it exists."

"What?" said Janet. "Husks just get together and . . . and . . . socialize?"

"I think so," said Sam. "It only lasts a few days at most, but the husks seem really to enjoy it. The precise location always seems to change. I think it's reasonable for us to guess that things might be the same way with the chrome huskies."

"This is nuts," said Sam. "What are we going to do?"

Mikaleh considered their predicament.

"Well, first things first—we can't wait days for their gathering to be over," she said. "I still don't know exactly what's happening with this key we're looking for. And I'm not exactly sure who wants what, and why they want it. But I think things are happening fast. I don't want to lose days waiting here. Or, frankly, by walking around them . . ."

"But . . ." Sam stammered.

"Did you see how wide that herd is?" Mikaleh said. "They go off into the canyons and you can't see where it ends. The chrome huskies out there are just the ones that we can see. We might walk for hours or days trying to circumvent a group this size."

"Uh-oh," said Sammy. "Then that only leaves . . ."

"Through," Mikaleh clarified. "And I think that's how we have to do it."

"I don't like to use the word 'impossible' very much," Sam began thoughtfully. "Usually, I reserve it for when Sammy is being frustrating, and even then I don't mean he's being literally impossible. But I've gotta say that this sounds a little bit like it might be *literally impossible.* Also dangerous. If those things notice us—like if one comes and peeks over the top of the hill and then goes and tells the others—our only option will be to run away. There are far too many for us to fight them, and they'll all chase after us."

"Yes, they will," Mikaleh said. "In fact, I'm kind of counting on that."

"Plan!" Janet suddenly shouted, while pointing at Mikaleh. It was as though she had identified a rare bird in the distance, and wanted to point it out to everyone before it flew away.

"What?" said Sam.

"Mikaleh has a plan!" Janet clarified. "That's the way she always talks when she does."

It was true. Mikaleh did have a plan. It would not be easy to execute, but no part of getting past an enormous herd of chrome huskies was going to be easy.

"If we can't get through the next valley because it's full of chrome huskies, then the solution is simple," Mikaleh said. "We get them to leave."

"What?" Janet said. "How? Just by going and yelling at them or something? I don't think that would work."

"No," Mikaleh said. "We're going to sort of funnel them. Away from the valley, and into a place that will be *very bad* for chrome huskies."

"How are we going to do that?" asked Janet.

"Think about when you're building defenses," Mikaleh said. "When you're anticipating an onslaught of husks of various types, the key is to keep them away from your base. You use walls to trip them up and get them stuck around the edges. Well, we're sort of going to do the opposite of that. We're going to build a long, high wall down each edge of the hill. The walls will be so long and so wide that the chrome huskies won't even notice them. At least not at first. But gradually, the walls will get narrower and narrower. We'll drive them to a single point."

"And at that single point will be . . . ?" Janet questioned. "I hope not us. Please don't say us."

"Not *exactly* us," Mikaleh said. "There's going to be a pen on the other side. As big as this whole valley on our side of the hill. If we can get the bulk of the chrome huskies into the pen, then we should be in good shape."

"This won't work," Sam said. "The first huskies to get through will just break down whatever fencing we build—even if we build it out of metal—when they realize they can't get out."

"Not if we put floor freeze traps all around the inside of the fence," Mikaleh said.

"Oh!" Sam said. "It'll be like a chrome husk–proof lining!"

"What?" Janet said. "How?"

"Chrome huskies don't go down for good unless you hit them with a fire or water weapon," Mikaleh said. "We've got a few of those in our arsenal, but not enough for a valley full of those things. But we can build floor freeze traps, which also do water damage."

"Ooh, we *could* do that," Janet said, seeing the point. "The first chrome huskies who tried to get through the walls would freeze, and then the other chrome huskies would be blocked by a layer of . . . dead chrome huskies."

"They disintegrate a bit after they die, but I'm thinking there would still be enough left for a nice firm layer," Mikaleh said.

"How strong is their chrome?" Sam asked, his mind busy with the figuring of it.

"You've fought chrome huskies before," Mikaleh said. "You tell me."

"From what I remember, it's pretty strong," Sam said.

"That's what I remember too," Mikaleh said with a smile.

"So what are we waiting for?" asked Janet. "Let's get to building!"

The group began by decimating nearby rocks and rock formations to harvest as much stone as they could. They all had a bit of wood in their inventories, but the squad knew the best approach was to work with the elements that were in the biome where you already were. It was the same principle that said a chef should always cook with local ingredients. Now and then, as they worked, Mikaleh hazarded glances up at the top of the hill. She still saw bright glintings whenever a chrome husky wandered near the top, but they seemed too distracted by their big party to wander across the top of the hill. Mikaleh hoped this situation would not change for the foreseeable future.

When enough stones had been harvested, the squad began building two parallel walls down the side of the sloping hill. Except the walls weren't perfectly parallel. They sloped in toward one another ever so slightly. It was difficult to notice this, which was just how Mikaleh wanted it. The squad worked as quickly as it could. Stone walls were not as quick to craft as wood. It would be easy to feel no sense of urgency at all, Mikaleh reckoned, but she also knew that the moment one of the chrome huskies chanced to look over the top of the hill, the plan was done for. Accordingly, they kept their heads down and worked fast.

Before long, the two walls had begun to narrow to a sort of tunnel.

"Keep it just wide enough that a single husky can pass through," Mikaleh said.

"I'm about husky-sized," Janet offered. "You can use me as your model."

As Janet slowly strode away from the hill and into the desert, Sam and Sammy crafted high stone walls on either side of her.

"Good," said Mikaleh. "Now widen it back up again. Here's where we build the pen."

The squad began opening the stone walls up to make the biggest enclosure any of them had ever built before.

"This is crazy," Sammy said. "You could fit a whole city in here. It would have its own zip code . . . if the world still had zip codes."

"I think they technically still exist," Sam offered. "It's just that nobody uses them anymore, on account of there being no mail service."

"Maybe we could start our own mail service when all this is over," Sammy said. "I always thought being a mailman would be fun."

"Suit yourself," Mikaleh interjected. "But for now, pretend you're a cattle rancher for a huge herd of cattle. But instead of actual cows, we're building a pen that will be filled with murderous, unstoppable, metal-coated huskies that want to eat us."

"Okay, but being a mail carrier is still my favorite job," said Sammy, continuing to craft the walls.

While the rest of her squad finished the enclosure—which really was big enough to hold a small town—Mikaleh began lining the inside of the walls with floor freeze traps. As leader of the best squad around, she had amassed quite a collection in her inventory. Now she knew why she'd saved them. Some were merely rare, some were positively epic, and some were so legendary that they would probably freeze a chrome husky if the creature merely looked at it. All of them, Mikaleh deployed around the walls with great care. Chrome huskies were resilient and mean, but they weren't smart. Mikaleh did nothing to conceal the trap plates. She knew that a husky in a hurry would simply lumber and stumble right into them.

Sam and Sammy eventually closed the loop on their wall, sealing the pen for good. The rest of the squad had a few floor freeze traps of their own, and helped Mikaleh finish the interior lining.

"So here is my question," Sammy said as they completed the final stretch. "What's going to get the chrome huskies interested in entering this pen in the first place?"

"I thought that part was obvious," Mikaleh said. "Us. We are."

"But . . . wait," Sammy said. "I can think of several problems with that. Okay, more like just one problem. But it's a really big one."

"Don't worry," said Mikaleh. "I have a plan. I've been working it out in my head while we've been laying these traps."

"You didn't have a plan *before* we started all this building?" Sam asked in disbelief.

"I had *most* of the plan then," Mikaleh confided. "But now I've got the other half. Sometimes you've got to think of things as you go. If I had to know everything before I got started, our squad would never get anything done."

"Okay," Sam said. "Well, now that you have it, do you mind enlightening the rest of us?"

"Not at all," she said, taking a seat in the dusty Canny Valley dirt. "Gather around and I'll explain. But listen carefully. If we don't pull this off just as I say, the entire thing's going be a disaster."

Mikaleh began to tell the squad her plan.

Several minutes later, Sammy found himself scaling the steep hill to where the horde of chrome huskies waited. He had several questions in his mind, but most of them started and ended with "Why me?" Then he remembered. *Oh. Because I'm a ninja. The speed and double jumps. Riiiiiiight.*

When he reached the crest of the hill, the valley on the far side of the hill spread out below him. It was now late afternoon, so the chrome huskies had had all day to soak up the summer sun. They positively radiated heat. The entire valley cooked. The chrome huskies seemed hardly to notice. Sammy, on the other hand, had to steady himself on his sword to avoid passing out from the heat.

With his free hand, Sammy reached into his inventory and took out an apple. He took a deep breath. He knew that he was about to pass the point of no return. The place from which there was no going back. If Mikaleh's plan didn't work, it might mean the end of all of them—but *especially* of all of *him*. But Mikaleh had never led her squad wrong in the past, and Sammy trusted her implicitly. He decided to trust her again.

Sammy took a deep breath and threw the apple.

It sailed through the air, hit one chrome husky on the head, and then skittered onto another husky's hot metal back where it immediately began to cook like an apple fritter.

The husky who had been struck on the head looked up. At first, Sammy was concerned it might not see him. The husky looked all around, wondering which of its friends was the wise guy and had struck him in the head.

Then it happened. The chrome husky's eyes locked like a laser on to Sammy.

For a moment, the great shiny behemoth only looked. Sammy hesitated, wondering if a second apple might be necessary. But then the chrome husky began to emit a long low grunt of alarm. (It sounded much like a regular husky, only chromier.)

The others turned to look, and they also saw Sammy peering over the top of the hill. Now the reaction was instantaneous. The entire herd took off after him at a good clip.

Needing no further prompting, Sammy sprinted back down the hill. The great shiny monsters followed. It looked, from a distance, as though a huge collection of pinballs had been unleashed down the side of the hill—with Sammy doing his best to avoid being run over by them.

Sammy made for the spot where the newly constructed walls narrowed to a point thin enough for only a single chrome husky to pass through. As he reached the narrow entrance that would open again into the larger pen, he just had time to shout: "This had better work."

And any pursuing chrome huskies could have been forgiven for thinking he was talking to himself. For there was nothing else to be seen beside the opening except three small bushes. The bushes looked as though they had been growing in that spot for many years. And as the chrome huskies passed them in a mad dash to catch up with Sammy, it was almost unnoticeable when one of them sneezed.

"Bless you," said the bush costume containing Sam.

"Thank you," said the one containing Janet.

"Be quiet," whispered the one containing Mikaleh. "They haven't all passed by yet!"

Very few chrome huskies heard these words, and those that did assumed they were coming from other huskies. One by one, the huskies entered the narrow sluice and emerged into the enormous pen on the other side. It took quite a while for such a large group to fit through. Mikaleh had worried that not all of the chrome huskies would take the bait, but she needn't have. True to form, every one of them had found Sammy completely irresistible. On and on they came, and soon all of them had passed into the pen beyond. Now Mikaleh's only concern was Sammy's ability to take evasive action while the rest of the squad pinned them in.

"Okay, they're through," Mikaleh said, sloughing off her bush costume. "We only have a few moments to pin them in. We should alternate between freeze floor traps and metal walls. Get 'em pinned in real good. When they realize they're trapped, they'll try to come back the way they came. We've got to make this the toughest point of all."

"Stand aside!" bellowed Janet. "I was born to do this!"

With help from Mikaleh and Sam, Janet began turning the sluice tunnel into a fortification of epic traps and walls. It was some of the finest construction work she'd ever done. (Janet, like all good constructors, worked well under pressure.) Within moments, she had built one of the most formidable blockades of her career. The chances of any chrome huskies—or anything else for that matter—getting through that tunnel inside of a day seemed doubtful to Mikaleh.

"There!" Janet said when the final piece of metal was in place. "My latest masterpiece. Mwah!" She kissed the tips of her fingers like a gourmand.

"Yes, that's excellent work," Mikaleh said. "So I suppose we should let Sammy know that he can jump over the wall now."

"Do you think he's all right in there?" Janet asked.

"He's fine," Sam said confidently. "Nobody can take evasive action better than Sammy. Plus, he was just saying the other day how he needed more exercise."

"Even so, I think his job is done," Mikaleh said.

She quickly constructed a wooden ramp leading up to the side of the pen. She walked halfway up it, just enough to see inside.

There, indeed, was Sammy. He was running wide circles around the outer edges of the pen. A great cluster of chrome huskies were chasing after him—like a mass of metal being drawn to a moving magnet. However, to Sammy's great advantage, the chrome huskies were not smart enough to realize that if he had come around the pen in a great arcing circle once, than he was liable to do it again. So instead of laying in wait for him to do another lap, the chrome huskies only chased the tail of the mob heading after him.

"It's sort of pretty in a weird way," Janet said, joining Mikaleh halfway up the ramp. "All that slow rotating metal. It's like the hand of a giant clock. Except that the hand is trying to catch Sammy and tear him to pieces."

"Pretty or not, I think Sammy deserves a rest now," Mikaleh said.

"Whatever you say, boss," said Janet.

Mikaleh began to jump and wave frantically.

"Hey, Sammy," she cried. "Over here!"

Even over the sound of hundreds of running chrome huskies, Sammy heard his boss's voice loud and clear. He changed course and began sprinting for the side of the wall where Mikaleh and Janet stood. As he neared it, he accelerated even further. Then he did a double jump and bounded over the wall.

"Only Sammy can jump like that," Mikaleh said, always impressed by what the ninja could do.

"Yeah," Janet agreed. "And even for him, that was pretty high."

Now, on the outside of the wall and safe from the chrome huskies, Sammy tried to catch his breath.

"That was exhausting," he said. "Did the plan work?"

"Why don't you join us on this ramp and take a look?" Mikaleh asked.

Sammy did. Sam walked onto the ramp too, and together the squad watched a very large group of very confused chrome huskies gradually realize there was no way out of the enormous pen. Then, far down the wall, they heard the distinctive sound of a freeze trap being triggered. Then another. And then another still. The creatures were beginning to realize that they were stuck.

"Now if you really wanted to have some fun, you could build a platform here and have fun taking these guys out with a sniper rife—Pew! Pew!" said Janet.

"That would be kinda fun," Mikaleh said. "If only we had the time. Keep in mind that our goal is to find the Traveler and get some answers about what's going on."

"I know," said Janet, sighing wistfully at the thought of picking off so many chrome huskies in such a tight space. "But a girl can dream, can't she?"

The squad left the enormous pen behind. As they walked away, the sound of freeze traps being triggered became a clamor.

"I feel weird about interrupting their big annual gathering," Sammy said.

"It would have felt weirder if they had caught you and eaten you though," Mikaleh assured him.

"Yeah," he said. "I suppose you're right about that."

The squad climbed the hill once more and gazed down into the valley formerly occupied by hundreds of chrome huskies. Everything below was trampled into chaos. What once might have been a pleasant valley was now quite decimated, and the chrome huskies had left detritus everywhere.

"That's the problem with big gatherings," Janet said. "They always leave places looking like *this* the next day."

"It's like how it looked after an outdoor concert in the time before the Storm," said Sammy.

The squad headed down into the valley. The landscape was littered with bits and bobs left behind. Most of it was just junk that would not be useful, but here and there they stopped to pick up an odd crafting component that looked promising. Sam even found an Active Powercell, which he quickly squirreled away, aiming to create a menacing weapon with it whenever he had some spare time.

As the squad reached the far side of the valley, a lone chrome husky toddled into view from a different direction, its chrome head gleaming in the sun.

"What's this?" Sammy said. "Did one of those things get out already?"

"No," said Janet. "It's come from a different direction. Look. I think it's just late to the party."

Sure enough, the chrome husky approached the empty valley with a mix of awe and surprise on its face. It made a slow inspection of the lip of the valley, then shrugged and walked away.

"Little does he know it's his lucky day," said Janet. "He just barely missed being locked up in a pen!"

Oblivious to his good fortune, the chrome husky wandered away into the desert. The squad ignored the solitary creature, and headed in the direction of the North Canny Valley Outpost.

CHAPTER SEVEN

Just a few hundred yards from the outpost, a strange sight came into view. Three people. Two men and a woman. At first, only their silhouettes were visible. All wore heavy clothes despite the dust and heat—though the shadows had grown long now, and sunset approached. The strangers standing on the outside of the trio—a man and a woman—were both armed with long guns of some kind. Yet it was the man in the middle that drew the squad's attention.

Sam and Sammy were the first to conjecture aloud.

"It's a washing tub of some sort," Sammy said. "A small one. Like for a pet."

"No," said Sam. "You're making it too complicated. It's a bucket."

"What if it's flowerpot for a really big flower?" Sammy tried again.

"I could see that," said Sam. "Do you think they cut holes so he can see?"

"Look at the way he stumbles, though," said Sammy. "I don't think they've cut eyeholes at all."

"You're right," Sam agreed. "Lookit how the other two have to guide him when he begins to go off course. That guy's walking blind!"

Mikaleh could not contain herself any longer.

"What *are* you talking about?" she said. "Those people headed our way?"

"Yeah," Sammy said. "One of them's got a . . . thing on his head. Or something."

"That's not a hat?" said Mikaleh.

Sammy and Sam both shook their heads no.

"We agree on that point," said Sam, "but . . . what is it?"

"Flowerpot," said Janet, squinting into the sunset. "Definitely a flowerpot. Or wait, no. Maybe it's a bucket. Now I see a bucket for sure."

Mikaleh rolled her eyes. They moved closer to the strange trio. The strange trio moved closer to them.

"Okay," said Mikaleh. "Now I'm curious. I think we should stop and talk to them."

"Right," said Sammy excitedly. "We've got to ask 'Is that a bucket or is that a flowerpot?'"

"Actually," said Mikaleh, "I'm more interested in asking why the person in the center has their hands tied."

Now that Mikaleh had pointed it out, the rest of the squad saw it too.

"Ooh, so he's a prisoner," said Janet. "I wonder what he did. He must be a really bad guy, especially if they had to tie his hands and put a bucket on his head."

"Or a flowerpot," said Sammy, hedging his bets.

The strange trio moved closer, and it became clear the two groups would meet. The man and woman kept their weapons at the ready. Their faces looked hard and tough.

Eventually, they got close enough that everyone could clearly see it was a bucket.

"Told ya," Sam said.

"Zip it," said Mikaleh.

The two groups drew close enough to speak.

The woman from the trio spoke first. Her tone was aggressive and bordered on rude.

"Don't get any ideas!" she cried. "I don't know if you're friendly or not, but all we have to do is whistle and all our friends from the North Canny Valley Outpost will come running to fight at our side."

Given that the outpost was still far in the distance, Mikaleh thought that this was a bit silly.

"What'd this guy do?" asked Janet. "Why do you have his hands tied and a bucket on his head?"

"It's a pail, actually," said the male captor.

"No, we're pretty certain it's a bucket," Janet told him.

"This one has been trouble for years," said the man. "We kicked him out ages ago, but he was trying to come back. He's always hanging around and causing trouble. Filling the heads of children with nonsense, and begging things off of people."

"And these are crimes?" Mikaleh said skeptically. "Seems like that's how a whole lot of people have been living since the Storm."

"We didn't used to think he was particularly harmful either," said the man. "But yesterday he stole my Active Powercell and chucked it right into the middle of a big gathering of chrome huskies. It was really inconsiderate."

"You were being a *jerk*," a voice said from underneath the bucket.

It was a voice that Mikaleh recognized immediately. It could only have belonged to the Traveler.

She hoped this fact had not registered on her face. When you were trying to get something from someone, Mikaleh knew it was best when they didn't know you wanted it at all.

"Well," Mikaleh said thoughtfully. "Throwing an Active Powercell away is certainly a lousy thing to do. Tell me, what's his punishment going to be."

The man and the woman smiled evilly.

"He's going to get it back from the chrome huskies," they said. "Whether he wants to or not."

Mikaleh and Sam exchanged a knowing glance.

"Gosh, it's a shame you have to walk all the way back to that chrome husky herd," Mikaleh said. "So this guy didn't just take your Active Powercell, he's now wasting a bunch of your time too by making you walk all that way."

"Ehh, we don't really mind," said the man. "We're so angry at him, it'll be worth it when we get to the part where we get to watch him try to get it back."

"Yeah," said the woman. "Maybe he'll try to sneak in and find it while they're asleep. But wait a minute, chrome huskies don't sleep! Stinks to be you, I guess, eh, bucket-head?"

Mikaleh said: "Yes, but wouldn't you rather just have your Active Powercell back?"

"I'd rather be twenty feet tall and have lasers for arms, but that ain't gonna happen," said the man. "What's the point in wishing?"

Mikaleh looked over at Sam.

"I've got some good news for you," Sam said. "Sometimes you do get what you want. We found your Active Powercell."

Sam reached into his inventory and gently tossed the item to the male captor. The man was so surprised, he nearly dropped his gun.

"What?" he said in confusion. "This *is* my Active Powercell. I scratched my name into the bottom just in case it ever got stolen. Where did you find this? *How* did you find this?"

"It was right where you said it was," said Mikaleh.

"Yep," said Sam. "In a field filled with hundreds and hundreds of chrome huskies."

The man's eyes went very wide. He looked the squad members up and down, as if meeting them again for the first time. "*You* did that?" he asked in astonishment.

"Sure," said Mikaleh, as if it were no big deal.

"Uh . . . well . . . thank you for returning my Active Powercell," the man said.

"Oh, I didn't say it was free," Mikaleh responded.

The man began to grow white with fear.

"I mean, it actually is free," Mikaleh continued. "But it would certainly be *nice* if you wanted to do something for us in return."

"Sure thing," said the man. "If it's in my power to give you, then it's yours. And if it's not in my power, I'll still see what I can do."

"Why don't you let *us* punish this jerk with the bucket over his head?" said Mikaleh. "Then you wouldn't have to worry about it anymore. And I think we'd be able to give him exactly what he deserves."

"Gladly," said the man.

"Yes, please take him off our hands," said the woman. "He's been nothing but trouble. He's really, really annoying. Plus, he also smells kind of weird."

"You'd smell weird too if somebody put a bucket on your head and left you in the hot sun," the Traveler retorted.

Mikaleh acted as though she did not hear this.

"Come along with us," Mikaleh said, gripping the Traveler ominously on the shoulder. "We'll teach you to be annoying and throw other people's property into a gathering of chrome huskies."

"Yeah," said Sam. "We'll teach you real good."

"Fine," said the Traveler defiantly. "One group of jerks is just as good as another. Lead on!"

The Traveler turned and faced the desert, as if he had some destination in mind.

His former captors happily began the journey back to the North Canny Valley Outpost.

"Here, come with us," Mikaleh said. She conducted the group to the cool shadow of a rock outcropping. Once behind it—and safely out of sight—she removed the Traveler's bucket and untied his hands.

"Here," she said. "Have some food and water from my inventory. Also, you should sit here in the shade and rest for a while. It looks like you've really been through it."

Though it had been some years since she had seen him, the Traveler did not appear to have changed one bit. His skin was old and tough as leather, and his hair was stark white and stuck up wildly in all directions. He also had the same wild look in his eye that was something of a trademark for him.

"Hey, I remember you," the Traveler said. "You used to come and roust me when I was hanging around your base too long. Now . . . which base was that? I move around so often that I have trouble remembering. I would always try to be helpful and tell you all the valuable things I know, but you guys never wanted to hear it. Is it because I look different from most survivors, with my spiky white hair? It *is* possible to look different and still be right about something, you know."

"We know," said Mikaleh. "In fact, we came all the way here to try to find you precisely because of the things *you* know. Really, one specific thing."

"Oh yeah?" said the Traveler, happily relaxing in the cool shade cast by the rocks. He began exploring the provisions Mikaleh had offered.

"Do you remember when you used to talk about the Last Survivor?" Mikaleh asked.

"Sure I do," said the Traveler, now eagerly chewing away. "It was one of my most popular stories. At least back in the day. I haven't told that one in a while. Stories are like songs. They get really popular for a while, but then people are suddenly sick of them. If you want to make a living as a traveling storyteller hobo, you have to grasp that idea pretty quickly."

"You're calling it a 'story,'" Mikaleh pointed out. "Does that mean it's not true? Because we might have some evidence to the contrary."

The Traveler chewed thoughtfully for a moment, considering the question.

"Stories, fables, legends . . ." he began. "They're all useful to me inasmuch as people—if they like hearing 'em—are liable to give me something to eat after I tell them. Some are real and true, and some are fake and didn't really happen. People just made 'em up. Heck, maybe *I* made 'em up. The point is, what's important to me isn't whether a story is true or not. If I had to go around remembering which of my stories were true and which were false, I'd never get anything else done."

"Do you remember who you heard the story from about the Last Survivor?" Sam asked, beginning to take notes.

The Traveler chewed some more.

"I don't reckon I do," he said. "It was one of the stories from the first days after the Storm came. Sometimes stories go around the hobo camps, and I catch 'em, like catching a cold."

"I see," said Sam, as though this were not a very satisfying answer.

Mikaleh said: "We have reason to believe that *that* particular story might be true. We met a husk who asked us to go and fetch a gold key with a red ruby handle from him."

"Ahh," said the Traveler. "Just like in the story."

"Uh-huh, but then it wasn't where he told us it would be," Mikaleh continued. "Then we learned some beehives had been looking for it. And they seemed to know a bit more about the key and how it was connected to the Last Survivor."

"Ah, the Last Survivor," the Traveler said, as if remembering fondly. "It's all coming back to me now. The Last Survivor was a thing of legend that—if ever found—had incredible powers that might make the difference in the fight against the husks."

"Yes," said Mikaleh. "But the beehives made it sound like the Last Survivor wasn't a thing, but a person."

The Traveler suddenly sat up violently, as if he had accidentally rolled over onto a cactus. His face showed a gradual, growing alarm.

"Wait a minute . . ." he said. "The story of the Last Survivor is all coming back to me now. And I'm not sure I like it. I always told myself that story was a work of fiction. It had to be. The possibility of it being true seemed too low. But now the four of you are telling me it actually is true!"

"Yes," Mikaleh said. "We're trying to figure out what's going on, and we need your help. We need you to tell us the story again, exactly as you used to tell it."

"Oh no," the Traveler said. "That would be far too unsettling and scary."

Janet spoke up.

"But . . . but . . . we just rescued you from almost certainly being mauled by a bunch of chrome huskies. And we gave you food and water."

"And for those things, I am mighty grateful," said the Traveler, letting out a burp. "But I still don't want to talk about that story."

"I'm a heck of a builder," Janet said. "What if I built you a nice big house to live in? Then would you tell us?"

The Traveler seemed to consider it for a moment, but remained unswayed.

"Naw," he said. "Moving around and telling stories is how I make my living. Staying in one place all the time would completely upend my business model. I don't think it's a very good idea."

"Well then, what would it take?" Janet asked.

The Traveler smiled from ear to ear.

"A hundred," he said.

"A hundred?" Janet repeated. "Like, a hundred dollars? People don't really use money much anymore, but I'm sure if we went wading through some garbage heaps—or the ruins of a bank—we might be able to find some cash."

The Traveler shook his head.

"A hundred apples," he said. "Food is the only currency with me. It's the only thing I want. Apples restore health and they're lightweight so I can carry a lot of them."

"Okay; a hundred is a lot, though," Janet said. "I mean, I'm sure we have *some* apples."

"Let's check, people," said Mikaleh. "Everybody open your inventories."

The squad began riffling through their possessions looking for apples. Whenever they found one, they tossed it on the ground at the Traveler's feet. The Traveler smiled and clapped his hands like a baby as the pile of fruit grew and grew. When the squad was done, Janet took a knee next to the pile and began counting.

"Forty-eight, forty-nine, fifty . . . *fifty-one!* Fifty-one apples. There you go."

"Wait," said the Traveler. "That one there has a worm in it. And it looks old. I don't like old, wormy apples."

"Fine, then," Janet said, removing the offending apple from the pile and tossing it into the desert.

"Fifty is not a hundred, though," said the Traveler. "You're only halfway there."

"Are you serious?" said Mikaleh.

"What?" said the Traveler. "It's not like they're that hard to find. There are apples in Tomato Town, for example."

"We are nowhere near Tomato Town, and you know it," said Janet.

"Fine," said the Traveler. "I guess I *do* know of some other apple trees that are sort of in the general area . . . and also aren't on an island full of crazy people trying to kill each other. Want me to just take you there?"

"Will you help pick the apples when we arrive?" Janet asked.

"No," the Traveler said. "But I'll be happy to watch you pick them. And I promise not to interfere with you picking them. That's about the best deal you're going to get from me."

Janet, Mikaleh, and Sam and Sammy all looked at one another. Was there any choice?

"You really think it's going to help us when he tells us that story again?" Janet whispered.

"I'm afraid I do," Mikaleh said. "And I also don't have a better lead for us to follow right now. Besides, picking apples can't be as hard as building a pen around hundreds of chrome huskies, which we just did. Compared to that, apples will be a cakewalk."

"I guess you're right," Janet said. "And I can build platforms to help us get any apples that are up high and haven't fallen out of the tree yet."

"Good," said Mikaleh. "And plus, it's just fifty of them. How long can that even take?"

They turned back to the Traveler, who was still relaxing in the shade.

"Fine," said Janet. "If there really is a forest with apple trees close by, take us to it."

"Great," said the Traveler. "It's a walk. Not too far. Less than half an hour. I don't suppose you all would considering carrying me, just the same."

"That's a hard no," said Mikaleh.

"All right," said the Traveler. "You can't blame a guy for trying. If you're ready, then follow me."

And the strange storyteller led them off across the sandy desert toward a forest.

At least, that was what the squad hoped.

CHAPTER EIGHT

Y ou've got to see it from my point of view," the Traveler said, ducking under a branch. They had walked for miles, and were not—properly speaking—even in Canny Valley anymore. They were, however, in a forest that seemed to abut it. All things considered, Mikaleh decided that the forest being real counted as a small victory.

"What's your point of view, then?" Janet asked. "Tell me. It will break the monotony while you look for the apple trees."

"Stories are how I make my living," said the Traveler. "If I tell it to all of you—the whole version, with *all* the details—then what's to stop you from going around and telling it yourself? It'll saturate the market. Then nobody'll want to hear it. This hundred apples is payment against all the future tellings that I won't be able to do."

"Waaaaait," said Janet. "I thought you said before that this was an old story that you'd stopped telling. And also, that you didn't even know if it was true."

"Did I say that?" the Traveler replied evasively. "Stories can have resurgences and get popular again. It's like songs. At first they're popular, then everybody is sick of them, then they come back as an 'oldie.' Circle of life."

The Traveler burped, as if to accentuate his point.

"Uh-*huh*," Janet said, her emphasis indicating that she did not quite believe this.

"Anyhow, we're close now," said the Traveler. "Look!"

The squad looked. There were indeed apples on the tops of some of the trees, and a couple of apples on the ground.

"Okay, finally," Mikaleh said. "We'll start picking these apples. C'mon. Let's get it over with. We've wasted enough time already."

"No . . . wait!" said the Traveler.

The squad looked at him oddly. It didn't seem right that he should be so alarmed.

"Uh, what I mean is, there are even better apple trees with way more fruit on them a little deeper into the forest," he quickly added.

"Hold on," said Mikaleh. "What is this? Are you leading us into some sort of trap?"

"I feel like everything's a trap these days," said Janet. "Just the way of the world after the Storm, I guess."

"No traps, I promise," the Traveler said. "Now follow me."

Showing surprising speed, the storyteller picked up his pace and headed deeper into the forest. The squad followed warily. True to his forecasting, the apples did grow denser and thicker as they moved farther in. After another fifty yards, all the trees were apple trees.

"Wow, you weren't kidding," said Janet.

"Yes," the Traveler cried. "But the best apples of all grow here in the center of the forest. Just a little bit more."

Now Mikaleh was suspicious. She took an assault rifle out of her inventory and shouldered it. The rest of the squad also drew their weapons.

The Traveler had passed out of sight through the trees, but they heard him call: "Ahh. Now *here* are the apples we want. Yes sir. These are certainly the finest. Come take a look."

Cautiously, with Mikaleh in the lead, the squad followed the Traveler's voice. There, in the center of the forest, they found a clearing filled with apple trees. The biggest, reddest apples any of them had ever seen. Mikaleh reckoned that their health-restoring capabilities must have been prodigious.

Yet the apples were not what held Mikaleh's attention. This was because, at the dead center of the clearing, resting against the foot of the largest apple tree, were several treasure chests. They glowed as if they could hardly contain the special items held inside. They had been placed all around the tree, almost as if they were fruit that had fallen down.

(Mikaleh would be loath to admit it later, but she had even risked a glance up into the branches to make sure they had not discovered some new form of "treasure tree." But no, they hadn't. The tree's branches held only fruit.)

"What the heck is this?" Janet boomed, saying what all of them were thinking. "There's a huge treasure hoard inside of this orchard!"

"Oh," the Traveler said, as though he were not very interested at all. "So there is."

"Was this always here?" Janet pressed. "Does it belong to anybody?"

"I'm really more concerned about apples," said the Traveler. "Chests mostly hold weapons and building materials. Neither of those things is useful to me. I've never been a fighter, and learning to build stuff always seemed like too much work. I just avoid those categories of activity altogether."

"I can't believe you're not curious!" said Janet. "Just look at all this loot!"

Janet charged forward toward the nearest chest.

"Janet, wait!" was all that Mikaleh had time to say.

Before Janet knew what was happening, one of the chests had sprouted legs. Then arms. Then it stood up and began to lumber in Janet's direction. The lid of the chest opened very much like a menacing, hungry mouth.

Janet jumped back out of the way and reached for her sledgehammer.

"They're mimics!" Mikaleh warned. "All of them."

As the squad looked on, more and more of the chests began sprouting appendages and opening their lids hungrily. The creatures had not eaten in a very long time and were ravenous. They came at the squad full tilt.

"You guys know what to do!" Mikaleh shouted. They did.

Mikaleh hit the advancing mimics with a spray from her legendary assault rifle. Several went down, but the rest kept coming. One mimic peeled off to the side as though it would flank the squad. Janet made short work of it with her hammer, hitting it again and again until it stopped moving. Meanwhile, Sammy charged forward and did a double-jump over the walking chests, landing at the very rear of the group. This was his favorite tactic. Before the mimics could realize what had happened, Sammy began cutting them down with his sword. Sam pulled an automatic shotgun from his inventory and waded forward, shooting madly.

The sound of their weapons discharging shook the quiet forest. Small animals leapt out of their holes and headed for cover. Bits of bark were blasted from the nearby trees. Apples fell left and right and were quickly squashed underfoot.

One by one, the mimics went down. They did not get back up again. The base of the tree was soon a tangle of their bodies.

Mikaleh scanned the horizontal mimics, waiting for one of them to twitch. When none of them did, she put her weapon away. The rest of the squad followed suit.

"Everybody okay?" she called.

There were nods all around.

"I'm sort of covered in apple juice," Sammy said. "But if you've got to be covered by *something* after a battle, apple juice is probably a good option."

Now that she knew her squad was safe, Mikaleh's thoughts turned back to the Traveler, and her blood ran hot. She spun around, expecting to see that he had run away. Instead, he stood where he was, an expression of pleasure on his face.

"How could you?" Mikaleh said. "After all we did for you, you do . . . *this*? We rescue you from being thrown to the chrome huskies, and you throw us to the mimics? That's a lousy thing to do. You didn't even really care about the apples in the first place, did you?"

"Not really," the Traveler said. "But I might as well be honest with you. There's something here that's much more valuable than apples."

The Traveler walked over to the slowly evaporating bodies of the defeated mimics. He began picking his way through them, and started pulling some away from a pile. This soon revealed one last glowing chest, resting beneath the heap.

"One more mimic we missed?" Janet said. "If you're not careful, it'll jump up and get you."

"No, it won't," said the Traveler, opening the chest. "Because this one is real."

"Whatever's inside ought to be good, if you have to fight your way through all these mimics to get it," Sammy said idly.

"Oh, yes," said the Traveler. "It's about the best of all."

The Traveler reached into the chest and took something out. Then he stood, turned around, and held it high for the entire squad to see. It was a small golden key with a red-ruby handle.

"What!?" was all Mikaleh could say. (She was not sure if this was a question or an answer.)

"Yes," the Traveler said. "This is the key that husks are looking for. And mist monsters. And now, apparently, surviving humans too."

"I don't understand what's going on right now," Mikaleh admitted.

"That's okay," said the Traveler. "In a second, you will. I think I've got some explaining to do."

The Traveler sat himself down on the lid of the one real chest. Mikaleh and her squad gathered around like children at story time, sitting on the forest floor.

"First of all," the Traveler said, "allow me to begin by apologizing for the mimics. You see, some years ago, this key came into my possession, and I needed to hide it. More specifically, I needed to keep the key secret and safe—even from myself. I learned of this spot in the center of an apple orchard, where a cluster of mimics rested. I placed this key into a real chest, and tossed it in among the cluster of mimics. They all look so similar, pretty soon even I forgot which was which. That was kind of the point. I didn't want to be able to change my mind and retrieve the key myself. I also didn't want anyone to be able to force me to give it to them. However, I knew that one day, someone—or some group of people— might come along who was tough enough, determined enough, and ready for what was within. So these mimics were a kind of test. A test—I hasten to add—that you have just passed."

"Sweet," said Janet. "I was so bad at passing tests in school, but that one was no problem!"

The Traveler smiled mysteriously.

"If only you knew," he said. "For the real test is just about to begin."

Janet's face fell.

"Oof," she said. "I don't like the sound of that."

"This key is the key that can unlock the Last Survivor," said the Traveler. "And now I give it to you."

The Traveler reached out and offered the key to the squad. The rest of the squad members looked at Mikaleh. She carefully reached out and took it.

"You still need to tell us more, though," Mikaleh said, securing the key in her inventory. "Who is the Last Survivor, and why are people looking for him? Well, it's mostly husks, I guess. Or at least one husk with a droopy neck."

"As you all know, several short years ago the Storm came," said the Traveler. "But few alive today really understand what that meant. Few understand what exactly happened. Well, I'll tell you what happened. Two worlds came together. Our world, and the world of the husks—the world that hurts just to stand inside of for even a 'one-Mississippi.' It was Earth and the Storm world, crashing into each other."

Janet could not resist and raised her hand like they were students in class.

"So, um, do you mean another planet crashed into Earth?" she asked.

"No," said the Traveler, shaking his head gravely. "I mean that our dimension intersected with theirs. The cause of that intersection is unknown. It could have been scientists smashing particles in an underground lab. It could have been experiments to create mini–black holes. Or humans could be entirely innocent—and it could be something the husks did on their end that brought our worlds together in this nasty combination."

"I kind of doubt that," said Janet. "I don't think there are anything like 'husk scientists' doing experiments."

"The more you know of the husks, the more surprised you will be," the Traveler said. "But when our world and their world intersected, it was a violent event. Buildings were destroyed. Landscapes were rearranged. And many lives were lost. From what I have been able to gather, when our two worlds joined, it was catastrophic for the husk home world. Many were lost. The coming together of worlds had weeded out the weak. Only the most supernaturally strong survived. And that is how it happened."

"Wait . . ." said Sam, looking up from the notes he was feverishly taking. "You're saying that the Last Survivor is . . ."

"A husk."

It was Mikaleh who had spoken. It was all beginning to make sense to her. Part of it, anyway.

"Yes, that's right," said the Traveler. "The husks call him the Last Survivor because he was the only one to survive at the conjunction point of our worlds. And he's not just any husk. He is the most powerful husk ever to exist."

"So, he's got to be a hundred feet tall then, right?" said Sammy. "Maybe two hundred?"

The Traveler shook his head.

"I have heard that outwardly he appears to be a normal husk, as regular as the ones squads like yours mow down day in and day out. But he is also possessed of an immense power. He was made strong by the coming together of our two worlds at the most violent axis point. It transformed him into the ultimate husk. The Ur husk. The stories of his specific powers are hard to believe. He can withstand bullets and explosives and knives. He can throw an enemy a hundred years with the flick of his hand. He can control the very Storm itself, unleashing its power."

The Traveler paused dramatically to let this sink in.

The squad, however, was not entirely impressed.

"Even if you were up against something that powerful, there would still be ways around it," said Sam.

"Oh, sure," said Janet brightly. "You could still defeat him with trickery. You could fool it. Or, I don't know, confuse it into using its own powers against itself."

"Exactly," said Sam. "A lot of options would still be available."

The Traveler smiled and clapped his hands like a baby once more.

"Oh, good!" he said. "My instincts were right. I *have* selected the right squad for this job."

"What do you mean by that?" Mikaleh asked cautiously.

"Perhaps you have already guessed what happened to him," said the Traveler. "When most people first hear about the Last Survivor, they ask why the husks didn't use his incredible power to eliminate all the remaining humans and win every battle against us. But it is the cannier, cleverer humans who realize what the husks eventually did. Namely, that they realized it is too dangerous for either side to have something so powerful as the Last Survivor out there walking around. It's dangerous to humans, and also potentially to husks. Because they knew this, the husk leadership made plans to ensure the Last Survivor would be controlled."

"I'm guessing we're getting close to where the gold key with the red ruby handle comes in," Mikaleh stated.

"You guess correctly," the Traveler said. "The most powerful husks and mist monsters have imprisoned him in the most dangerous and forbidding part of Twine Peaks."

"Ooh, that must be *pretty* forbidding, then," said Janet. "Because all of Twine Peaks is forbidding, as far as I can tell. And dangerous. Dangerous goes without saying."

"Do you mind?" said the Traveler.

"Sorry," said Janet.

"There is a fortress of obsidian in a lake of lava and covered with traps," said the Traveler. "It's supposed to be hidden in the most terrifying part of Twine Peaks. The Last Survivor is locked inside of it."

"I see," said Mikaleh.

"This key was smuggled out," the Traveler explained. "It—and only it—has the ability to free him. As you might imagine, the Last Survivor is a divisive figure from the husks' point of view. Some husks think this war against the humans is taking too long, and that the Last Survivor should be freed and forced to use his power on their behalf. Other husks believe that releasing the Last Survivor would only give him an opportunity to revenge himself against the very husks who imprisoned him. That is, he might do our job for us, and eliminate every husk he could find. Yet today, few husks know about the Last Survivor, and fewer still know that the key to his cell has been lost. It is to the advantage of almost everybody involved that he should be forgotten, or his tale thought to be a mere legend. That's why I stopped telling that story in the first place. But even so, it's clear that there are some who are never going to forget, and never going to give up until they release him. The husk you spoke about—the one with the droop to his neck—is known to me. That is to say, I don't know him well, but I know that he is looking for the Lone

Survivor, and has been for some time. I do not know for sure, but I believe he is one of the proponents of freeing the Last Survivor to use him against the humans. He has been at it for as long as I can remember. But if he has gotten desperate enough to risk seeking the help of humans, then his desire is extreme indeed. Tell me, what did he promise you if you helped him?"

"Actually, he didn't totally say," Mikaleh admitted. "He made it sound like it would be a good gift we'd really like. To be totally honest with you, we mostly just took the job because it sounded like an adventure."

"Ahh," said the Traveler thoughtfully. "Interesting. This husk with the drooping neck . . ."

"We just call him Droopy," Mikaleh interjected.

"Very well then," said the Traveler. "This 'Droopy' scares the husk leadership. Many are working to stop him and recover the key before he can. Now, it seems as though they are racing against one another."

The Traveler paused for a moment, as if considering his next words carefully.

"I think," he said, "that the time has come to do what I had always hoped would never be necessary. And that is, to eliminate the threat posed by the Last Survivor."

"Wait," said Janet, sitting up very straight. "Why do we want to do that?"

"If there is even a *chance* of the Last Survivor falling into the hands of the one you call Droopy, then steps must be taken to prevent it," said the Traveler. "If the Last Survivor can be convinced to fight for the husks, then things would bode very poorly for humanity indeed. And even if the Last

Survivor turned on the husks themselves, out of anger, which many think he will . . . what then? What will he do after he has destroyed his captors and revenged himself? I do not think years of captivity and stewing in anger will have made him a friendly person when it comes to dealing with humans."

"I know I'd be angry," Janet said.

"No," the Traveler said. "I have been waiting for a squad that would be strong and clever enough to venture into Twine Peaks, navigate the fortress of lava, and do what needs to be done."

Mikaleh, who had been thinking deeply about all of this, took a breath and said: "Okay, two things. Number one, it sounds like this Last Survivor guy—even if he is a husk—is sort of a victim in all this. He didn't ask to be so powerful. And if the other husks don't like him, then maybe he's our friend. We attack husks because they attack us. If husks were peaceful, we wouldn't go around shooting them all day."

The Traveler opened his mouth to speak, but Mikaleh kept talking.

"And number two, if this guy is so tough, what makes you think we could defeat him if we wanted to? We're about the toughest squad there is—we've got the best weapons and gear, and our talents are unmatched—but we're not, you know . . . supernatural. It sounds like the Last Survivor could just use his powers to obliterate us before we got any licks in of our own, so to speak."

The Traveler opened his mouth to ask if she was done.

"Yes," Mikaleh said. "You can talk now."

The Traveler smiled a knowing smile.

"Thank you," he said. "You make very good points. I see that in addition to being strong and talented, you are also wise. Truly, I have chosen well. To your first point, I did not say that you will need to fight the Last Survivor to the death. I said that you will need to eliminate the threat he poses. If you can do this without violence, so much the better. I leave it up to you. Please take whatever approach you like. Now, when it comes to the 'how' of it all, there is one more thing you need to know about the Last Survivor. Take a hard look at the key in your hands."

"Okay," Mikaleh said. "I'm looking at it."

"Look at the handle," said the Traveler, "rather, look at what is *called* a ruby handle."

"Are you hinting that it's a fake ruby?" Mikaleh said. "Because I don't know rubies at all. I'm not a . . . not a . . ."

"Gemologist?" said Sam.

"Yes, that's right," said Mikaleh. "It's all the same to me."

"Well, if you *did* know rubies," said the Traveler, "you would know that the color of the one set into the key's handle is a bit wrong. Yes, it skews just a bit more purple than it ought to. This is because it is not a ruby at all, but the eye of a blaster that was shooting its blast attack just at the moment our worlds collided. The eye was crystallized in the explosion."

"That's something's *eye*?" Janet said doubt-fully. "Ew."

"Perhaps because it is also an anomaly caused by the coming together of worlds, this is the only weapon known to be effective against the Last Survivor," said the Traveler. "When it is near, his powers are diminished. This is why it was set into the key to his cell. His jailers would always be kept safe from their prisoner within. You see, in your hands is not only the power to free the Last Survivor. You also hold—if you so choose— the power to render him mortal and defeat him."

"Huh," said Janet. "And I thought it was just a decorated key. Shows what I know."

"Yes," said the Traveler. "It is, of course, much more than that. The key to the Last Survivor's cell is the key to defeating him. But . . . I have said all that I can, and I have given you all that I can. The rest, my friends, is up to you."

The squad looked at one another; then they all looked at Mikaleh.

"So you're saying that we can go now?" Mikaleh said with a grin. "Because this has been a lot more yapping and a lot less shooting than my squad is used to."

"Yes," said the Traveler. "Don't mind me. I think I'll sit here and eat some apples for a while. After that, who knows? I hear that Plankerton is hard-up for wandering storytellers at the moment. Maybe I'll give it a spin."

"I see," Mikaleh said. "At least we'll know where to find you. Last question then. How will we find this lava fortress, or whatever? We've been to Twine Peaks plenty of times, and I've never seen anything like that."

"Yeah," said Janet. "Also, it stinks there—but figuratively and literally. It's the last place I'd want to go poking around."

"Oh, you'll find it," the Traveler said, reaching for the nearest apple. "Just keep walking to where it looks like it might get more lava-y and more fortress-y. Walk to whichever place looks most unpleasant. Trust me. You won't be able to miss it."

"Okay then," Mikaleh said. "Thank you for trusting us with this."

"I just hope I've made the right choice," said the Traveler. "And if I haven't—and you're not up to the task—it'll only mean the potential release of a possibly crazy and angry all-powerful monster. So, you know . . . no worries."

CHAPTER NINE

They left the Traveler behind in the apple grove and headed back to the desert landscape of Canny Valley. The trees gradually gave way to grasslands, and the grasslands to desert. Soon there was only rock and sand beneath their feet.

"Are we far enough away to talk about what just happened?" Janet said.

"I hope we are," added Sammy. "But I have the feeling that the Traveler is the kind of guy who could just suddenly pop up behind a boulder."

"I don't see any boulders around here," said Sam. "It's flat."

"I don't know," Sammy said. "Maybe he could hide in a hole."

Mikaleh stopped walking and took out the key with the handle of red ruby that was not actually ruby at all. Night had gradually descended, and now she stared at it in the soft glow of the moonlight.

Mikaleh had wanted to get some distance between her squad and the Traveler, but there was a mental distance she needed too. The Traveler's story was a lot to take in. And if it were true, then the implications were powerful.

"My mother always used to say 'With great power comes great responsibility,'" Mikaleh said. "You ever hear that one?"

"Oh yeah," Janet said. "But I was never particularly powerful or responsible. So, as sayings go, it was never one of the ones that I thought about very much."

Mikaleh said: "I knew that we were probably the best squad in the world—whatever world this is now—but I never thought we'd have to do anything like this. Mostly, I was just having fun kicking butt and obliterating husks wherever we found them. But I guess it can't all be a party. This feels different now. I guess it's just been a long time since I've felt like something important was at stake."

"What do you mean?" said Janet. "I think beating up on husks is plenty important."

Mikaleh looked at Janet with the side of her eye.

"I think you know what I mean," Mikaleh said. "When was the last time you were really afraid that we'd lose a fight to the husks? Or that there would be serious consequences if we did? If we're out-fought or outgunned—which we haven't been in what seems like forever—we can always retreat to a safe distance. Fortifications can be rebuilt. Shields can be restored, even if the husks trash 'em. Those of us who have survived have gotten good at what we do. Heck, it's the reason why most of us have lasted this long in a world full of crazy monsters that want to eat us."

"I guess it has been a while since I was really afraid of anything the husks were going to throw at us," Janet said.

"And it's not a bad thing that we've gotten so good at our jobs," Mikaleh said. "It's just that this is . . . different. If what the Traveler is saying is true, then we really can't screw up. The fate of everything could be at stake."

Sam was typically a more analytical guy, so the whole squad noticed the emotional tremor in his voice.

"We're *not* going to screw up," he said. "We haven't worked this hard for nothing. We haven't developed our fighting and constructing skills to not use them. If there's a big job that needs to be done, I'm glad to be the one to do it."

Mikaleh smiled. "Do the rest of you feel the same way?" she asked.

They nodded in unison.

"Wow," Mikaleh said. "You guys inspire me. And I thought it was supposed to be the other way around. I'm the squad leader, so I'm supposed to inspire you."

"It can be a two-way street," Sammy opined.

"In that case, the only thing left to do is prepare," said Mikaleh. "I don't know if the Traveler told us everything—or if everything he told us is true—but going to investigate is the best way to find out. Obviously, we can't prepare for everything, but we should still do our best. What do we know about Twine Peaks?"

"Based on our previous trips there, I would say that first and foremost, it's awful," Janet said.

"Good," Mikaleh replied. "Elaborate."

"Sure," said Janet. "It's scary and gross and bleak. The landscape is gray and black. Except for the dangerous lava, which is bright red. And there's a lot of it. At least, a lot more than I'd like there to be. You can find every kind of husk skulking around there, even some weird ones like lobbers. And every single kind of mist monster. All in all, it's a pretty lousy place."

"I'm with you on that last point especially," Mikaleh said. "Boys, do you two have anything to add?"

"Just that you should watch out for flying lava and lava bombs," said Sammy.

"Yeah," agreed Sam. "Though sometimes you can use it to your advantage. Like by pushing one of your enemies into the lava."

"Yeah, I love that—Ker-splash!" said Sammy.

"Way to find a positive in a negative," said Mikaleh. "See, even lava can have its good points."

"I don't know about that," said Janet. "I hate lava almost as much as I hate bees."

"I'm a bit perplexed about the Traveler's suggestion that there could be a fortress in Twine Peaks that we've missed on our previous trips," said Mikaleh. "But then again, Twine Peaks isn't the sort of place where you 'hang around' when you're done with your mission."

"Yeah, lava's just not that much fun," said Sammy. "After you melt some things in it, you sort of run out of things to do. Seen one part of Twine Peaks, and you've seen it all."

"Except maybe you haven't," said Mikaleh. "Maybe you haven't seen all the parts of it because you never really wanted to look very hard. To a way of thinking, it might be the perfect place to conceal a fortress. From the Traveler's story, I get the feeling that the husks imprisoned the Last Survivor with an eye to him never getting out, and nobody ever getting him out. There'd be no reason for them to put his jail in an obvious place."

"Ick," said Janet. "We're going to have to go exploring in Twine Peaks, aren't we? This is really happening. How lousy."

"We could be exploring a field full of bees," Sammy offered.

"Hey, don't even joke about that," Janet said.

Mikaleh looked up at the sky, where clouds had begun to gather.

"Why don't we camp here for the night?" she suggested. "We've had a long day, and it looks like it's going to rain. We can head for Twine Peaks in the morning."

"Sounds good to me," said Sam.

"Same here," said Sammy. "I'm still exhausted from being chased by those chrome huskies."

"Janet, would you do the honors?" Mikaleh asked.

One of the great advantages of having a master builder in your squad was that you could pretty much have housing anywhere you wanted, at a moment's notice.

"What are you feeling tonight?" Janet asked, cracking her knuckles. "Ranch style? Duplex? Log cabin?"

"Surprise us," Mikaleh said.

While the rest of the squad got out of the way, Janet quickly threw up some walls on a giant square federal-style home. It was a fine combination of wood and brick, and even seemed to match the surrounding landscaping.

"Nice work!" Mikaleh said as Janet added the front door. "I don't see any husks out here, but you might want to add a trap or two for good measure."

"I always do," Janet said brightly.

Janet added several damage traps around the door and under the windows, and a launch pad trap around the rear just for good measure. (Anyone trying to sneak in the house's back door would be sent flying.) Inside the home, she set a cozy campfire into the middle of the floor, so the squad could huddle around and regain any health they had lost in the day's fighting.

"Thanks, Janet," Mikaleh said, taking her place beside the fire. "I recommend that everyone get to bed early tonight. All of us are going to have a big day tomorrow . . . the biggest day we've had in quite some time."

Later that night, Mikaleh rose from her spot by the campfire and climbed onto the roof of the building. It was a quiet night. The threatened rain had not come, but the sky was very dark with clouds. A cool wind blew. Across the desert landscape, she could hear the sand shifting.

She could also hear something else.

A few minutes later, Janet opened the rooftop door and joined her.

"Everything okay, boss?" she asked, taking a seat next to Mikaleh.

For a moment Mikaleh did not respond. She stayed very still, and her eyes remained trained across the darkened desert landscape.

Janet wondered if the squad leader was sleepwalking. Then Mikaleh whispered: "Look over there."

Janet did. The cool desert wind rustled the sand. Janet saw nothing. She wondered if she should pull out a sniper rifle scope.

Then she *did* see something. A movement so small that if she hadn't been looking for it, it would have been missed entirely.

In the distance, on the blue-black horizon of night, she saw a head . . . but like no head that Janet could recall seeing. Certainly, it could never be the head of a living human. It was irregularly rounded, and hung down at an unusual angle. In the front of it, two red eyes glowed grimly, like the last coals at the end of a fire.

"Husks!" Janet said. "They're preparing for a midnight ambush. These walls I've built will hold for a few minutes. I'll go and rouse the others."

Mikaleh shook her head no.

"Look again," she told her friend. "Not husks. Husk. Just one."

Janet looked again. It did seem to her that there were no other husks around it. Nothing else that looked even vaguely humanoid or husk-oid or anything. The two red eyes just lingered there in the distance alone, looking on.

"That's eerie," Janet said. "He's just standing over there spying on us. What a creeper."

"He has been following us, at least since we left the forest," said Mikaleh.

"He has?" said Janet.

Mikaleh nodded. "I saw him watching us from the trees. One of the reasons I wanted us to head back out to the desert is that it's harder to hide in this landscape. I knew that if he was truly fol-lowing us, he would have to give himself away sooner or later. And now he has."

"He's been out there all this time?" Janet asked.

"I think so," said Mikaleh. "Husks don't sleep."

"Why is *one* husk following us?" Janet said. "Why isn't he storming us and tearing up our base? Is he waiting for reinforcements?"

Mikaleh shrugged. "I've never seen a husk act this way," Mikaleh admitted. "But this week has been full of me seeing things that I never thought I'd see before."

"We could try to talk to him," Janet suggested.

"If he's still with us tomorrow, I'm going to do exactly that," Mikaleh said. "Now, why don't you go back down beside the cozy campfire and get some rest. I have a feeling we'll need all our strength in the morning."

"You sure you're okay up here by yourself?" Janet said.

Mikaleh looked at her as if to say: "It's *one* husk. What are you so worried about?"

"Okay, okay," Janet added as she began to descend the stairs. "I was just askin'. Gee. You try to be helpful . . ."

Janet's heavy tread got softer and softer as she moved back to the fire where Sam and Sammy slept. For her part, Mikaleh kept her eye on the horizon, watching the two red dots.

They watched her back.

The next morning the squad rose and collected their things. Janet noticed that Mikaleh had joined them down by the cozy campfire at some point. She wondered if the squad leader had really gotten any sleep.

"Want to smashy-smashy this place and collect the building components," Sammy asked brightly, stretching and taking out his pickaxe.

"Let's leave it in case some traveler coming this way needs a place to stay," Mikaleh said.

"Oh, that's a thoughtful gesture," Sammy said, putting his pickaxe back into his inventory. "Look at you being all considerate for the next group."

When they had packed up their things, they headed out across the desert landscape in the direction of Twine Peaks.

They walked for a good twenty minutes in silence before Janet said: "Gosh I'm so *not* looking forward to Twine Peaks. I know what we have to do is important and all; I just hate it there so much. It makes me stressed out to think about—and I can't stop thinking about it. My whole body is like 'No. Don't go there to that nasty lava place.' Seriously, my stomach hurts. My feet hurt. And I think my ears are reacting too because a second ago I thought I started to hear this weird high-pitched whine."

Mikaleh stopped walking. The others followed suit.

"Shhh," Mikaleh said. "Everybody listen."

"Listen for what?" Sam asked.

Mikaleh raised her hand to silence him.

"You won't be able to hear the whine in my head, silly," Janet said. "It's *inside my head*."

"Actually, I don't think it is," Mikaleh said.

They listened. A whine was discernibly approaching. Mikaleh looked up. The clouds had burned off with the dawn, and there was nothing but blue sky above.

In that blue sky was a human-shaped speck that seemed to be getting closer and closer at a very fast rate of speed. The whine that they heard was the mysterious shape yelling in alarm.

"Look out!" Mikaleh said.

"Why do I need to look—"

But that was all Janet had time to say.

A lone husk—very startled and upset—careened down from the sky and landed flat against Janet's back. Janet fell to the desert floor with an "Oof!" and there was a great puff of sand. When the sand cleared, Janet did a push-up to right herself, and the husk slid slowly and comically off her back.

"What's this?" Janet asked. "Flying husks now? It can't be!"

"Don't worry," Mikaleh said knowingly. "This one is only flying because he stepped on the giant bouncer trap I spent all night building on the roof of that house. I knew that any curious visitor who got too nosy would trigger it. And it looks like I got the angle just right."

Janet took a moment to glance back and forth between the house in the distance and the grumpy husk struggling to get back on its feet. Janet was, by far, the superior builder to Mikaleh, but she had to grant that, given enough time, her boss could pull off some pretty cool contraptions.

"Nice work," Janet allowed. "But did you have to make it so he would land on my back like that?"

"That was just a coincidence," Mikaleh said with a smile.

As a precaution, Sam and Sammy drew weapons, but neither expected the husk to attack.

Janet took a moment to inspect the husk as it righted itself and brushed away sand. After a few moments of righting, she realized it was as right as it was going to get. Which still left a decided droop to its appearance . . .

"Droopy!" Janet exclaimed.

The husk looked around the group, realized it was useless to lie, and grimly nodded.

"What are you doing here?" Janet asked. "Say . . . We've just learned from the Traveler that you're some kind of evil mastermind who wants to free the Last Survivor and use him to destroy humanity. I thought we were going to be in a race against you to see who could get to the Last Survivor first. But now you've just shown up here where we can smash you with a hammer. It's a little anticlimactic I'll grant, but it's certainly going to save us a lot of work."

Janet slowly drew her sledgehammer.

"Wait," said Droopy. "Please don't sledgehammer me just yet. We *are* still in a race, just not the way that you think."

"Eh, people will say anything to postpone being sledgehammered," Janet said, glancing at Mikaleh to see if she had the green light to swing away.

Mikaleh indicated that she should hold off for the moment.

"Droopy, why are you following us?" asked Mikaleh.

"I started following you because I thought you might be on your way to find the gold key with the red ruby handle, and I was right! But look . . . Back before, when I told you I thought it was in that cave with Grumpy Joe, I was telling the truth. I hear all kinds of rumors about where the key might be. It's been my project to find it for I don't know how long. I really thought I had a reliable source this time. I guess I didn't. *Like always . . .* But then I got the idea that you might try to find it on your own. And I was correct about that! I don't know why I didn't think of that earlier, actually. The greatest squad of humans would obviously be good for more than fighting and building. They'd be good at finding things. Anyhow, I watched from the forest when you defeated all those mimics and got the key. Then I followed you here."

Sammy stepped forward, his glistening sword shining in the morning sun.

"And you thought you would take it from us and use it to free the Last Survivor?" Sammy said. "Not going to happen!"

"Yes," Sam added, a bit more dispassionately. "Plus, there's no way you could take on the four of us. Even if you had a battalion of husks hiding over the next sand dune, I think we'd still win."

"There are no other husks," Droopy said. "There's just me. And I'm not here to fight you. I'm sorry I wasn't really honest with you before. But now I'm ready to be."

"I had the feeling there was more to this," Mikaleh said.

Droopy nodded.

"It's true that the Last Survivor is a husk with incredible powers that could be used against humans, or potentially against the husks ourselves," said Droopy. "And it's true—as far as I know—that the crystallized eye in that key seems to be the only thing that brings his powers under control. But the most important thing about the Last Survivor is . . . well . . . that he's my brother."

"What?" said Sam.

"I know it might sound unbelievable," Droopy began, "but that's why—"

"Husks have *brothers*?" Sam interjected. "We had no inkling that they were even related in the proper sense! What about sisters?"

"Uh, some of us do," said Droopy. "Not me though. I only have a brother."

"So the Last Survivor is your brother?" Mikaleh said. "That's why you're doing all of this."

"I miss him," Droopy said. "In the time before all of this happened—and our world and your world got mixed up—I got to hang out with my brother and do fun husk activities all the time. It was great. But when the worlds collided, he got affected in this weird way. So the senior husks and mist monsters locked him up. Just because they were afraid of him. I don't think it's fair. He doesn't deserve to be locked up, just for being different. I care about my brother, and I want to help him."

Mikaleh wondered: "So now you're asking us to . . . what? Give you the key?"

"No," said Droopy. "I'm asking if I can come with you."

Mikaleh had not expected this.

"Look, I can be helpful," Droopy said. "Especially in the bit at the end—that is, when we eventually do find my brother. I can convince him not to use his powers to hurt anybody. Not husks, but not humans either. Isn't a peaceful resolution always the best thing?"

Droopy looked at Mikaleh imploringly. She wondered if he was acting.

"And what if your brother turns out to be a real jerk?" Mikaleh asked. "What if he wants to use his powers to hurt as many people as he can? In that case, it's going to be our duty to make sure he doesn't. He'll be vulnerable while we have this key. We might have to take the opportunity to stop him in a very permanent way. Are you going to be able to handle that?"

"Hey, I'm not a monster!" Droopy said defensively. "Wait . . . I take that back. I am *technically* a monster, based on my understanding of how you humans use that word. But I'm not going to let anybody destroy the world, not even my own brother. All I'm asking is for you to give me a chance here."

Mikaleh surveyed her squad.

"This decision is bigger than just me," she said. "Droopy, go stand over there so we can talk."

"Happily," Droopy said, and loped a few paces away into the desert.

Mikaleh and her team huddled up.

"This is very strange," Sammy said. "I'm not sure how to feel."

"Droopy lied to us before," Janet observed. "What's to stop him from lying to us again? I think he's a liar then, and a liar now."

"If this *is* another deception, it is a very strange one," said Sam. "Personally, I'm inclined to trust him. However, I realize that my judgment may be clouded by my desire to interact for an extended period with a husk I can talk to. The research value would be immense. But it's not worth it if doing so means putting our squad in danger."

Then Sam, Sammy, and Janet looked at Mikaleh. She knew how they felt now. What was the squad leader going to say?

"This story is quite suspicious, and we know that Droopy is a liar because he lied to us before," Mikaleh began.

"So you agree with me then?" Janet said. "Good."

Mikaleh added: "Not necessarily. A liar can sometimes tell the truth, just like a stopped clock can be right twice a day. Also, some people lie because they're evil, bad people with no morals, for example . . . but sometimes other types of people tell a lie just because they're scared or they think they have no other options. If my own brother was in trouble, I might be tempted to tell a little fib if I thought it was the only way I could save him."

"Hmm," said Janet. "I still think liars are bad people most of the time."

"Sam, you're a smart guy," Mikaleh said. "What if you could devise some sort of test to see if Droopy is telling the truth?"

"That's a great idea!" Sam said brightly, but then his face fell. "Except . . ."

"Except what?" said Mikaleh.

"Except I don't know of any tests to see if somebody is telling the truth," he answered. "Even if we had an actual lie detector machine right here in front of us, I don't know if it would work because they measure heartbeat and brainwaves and other things that a husk might not even have."

"We're at a very important juncture," Mikaleh said. "Think, Sam. Is there a way we can tell if Droopy is telling the truth?"

Sam's face screwed up into a strange grimace to show that he was thinking hard.

"No," he finally said.

The rest of the squad sagged their shoulders in disappointment.

"But . . ." Sam added.

The squad straightened back up again.

"But it might be possible to devise one if I can have a while to think about it," Sam said.

Janet threw up her hands in frustration.

"We don't have a while!" she said. "We need to make a decision now."

Mikaleh turned her head to the side and narrowed her eyes.

"Actually . . . do we?" she said. "Think about it. What if we bring Droopy along while we walk toward Twine Peaks? What does that cost us? Sam can think of a suitable test while we walk. And if he doesn't think of one—or if we change our minds about Droopy—we can just tell him to get lost. What's the harm done?"

"That could work," Sam said. "If I can just ponder for a few hours—a day at most—I bet I can think of a really good truth-telling test."

"Gee, I don't know how I feel about this," Janet said.

"Tell you what," Mikaleh proposed, "you can walk directly behind Droopy the whole time, with your sledgehammer raised. The moment he gets out of line or does something bad, you can bonk him on the head."

"Okay," Janet said after a moment's consideration. "But it'll be a really hard bonk. No tippy-taps."

"Good," said Mikaleh. "Then we're in agreement."

Mikaleh turned to where Droopy toed the sand aimlessly several paces away.

"You can come back now!" she called to him.

Droopy scuttled over, an anxious look on his face. What had the squad decided?

"We're going to let you come with us to Twine Peaks," Mikaleh said. "But be clear . . . This doesn't mean that we trust you. This doesn't mean that we believe your story. And this certainly doesn't mean that we forgive you for lying to us back at the beginning of this whole mess. All it means is that you can come with us . . . for now."

"Oh, thank you so much!" said Droopy. "You're making the right decision. Everything I've said from this point out is true. You'll see when we meet my brother."

"For your sake, you better be right," Janet said, taking a position behind Droopy and raising her sledgehammer. "Now march!"

Droopy began marching across the sand like a soldier on parade.

Janet smiled. "At least he follows orders," she said.

"Yeah, let's see how long that lasts," Mikaleh said cautiously.

Forming a line behind Droopy, the squad headed out across the desert and in the direction of Twine Peaks.

CHAPTER TEN

You could smell it before you saw it. Twine Peaks was a place of burning and fire and stench. It radiated heat—not enough to cause damage, but enough to make you darn sure you weren't going to plan your next vacation there. In many places, the lava flowed underground just under the surface. The heat could radiate up through your feet. In Twine Peaks, it was a bad idea to stay in one place for very long. In Twine Peaks, everybody kept moving.

The squad had walked all day, and night had fallen. After having long announced itself on the wind, Twine Peaks came into view in the distance as a mass of purple and red and black. Lava flows lit up the night sky and shot up sparks, making the region seem like a giant foundry that covered the landscape. There were few trees or boulders, but great black rock formations jutted up into the sky at regular intervals. It created an uneven landscape with plenty of places to take cover and hide. This meant you could hide from monsters, but also that monsters could hide to ambush you. Every outcropping or giant boulder presented an opportunity for danger.

The presence of the Storm was strong. Lightning crackled in the sky, making shadows appear to move, and suddenly illuminating landscapes that had been dark a moment ago. In all its horribleness, the landscape of Twine Peaks was abruptly revealed in these flashes.

"Yeah," said Mikaleh. "This is probably where I'd build a prison to hold somebody I really didn't like."

She glanced back at Sam who walked behind her.

"So . . ." she said. "Have you thought of any . . .? You know."

"No," said Sam. "I'm still working on it."

"Work faster if you can," Mikaleh told him. "We're already almost here."

There was a sudden, extremely bright flash of lightning, and Mikaleh noticed a string of humanoid shapes peering over the edge of an outcropping that loomed high in the distance. They were stout, like huskies, but carried metal tanks on their shoulders. Every few moments, one of them seemed to shift its tank from shoulder to shoulder. After peering at the squad silently for several moments, the creatures slunk away.

"'Sploders," Janet said.

"Yes," said Mikaleh, arriving at the same conclusion. "I think we're still well out of range, but we should probably spread out to make ourselves harder targets for them."

"Yes," said Sammy. "Or at least not march in a line like British soldiers in the Revolutionary War."

"Okay," said Janet, as she turned to Droopy. "But any funny business, and you have my word that I will find you and whack you."

"I believe you," Droopy said fearfully.

The squad slowly spread out.

"I've seen 'sploders here before, but never that many," Droopy said to the group. "They must be getting more organized. Forming bands. Or maybe they're here as guards."

"Do you come here very much, looking for your brother?" Mikaleh asked.

"No," said Droopy. "It's been a long time since I've been back. I figured it was pointless to try to break him out without the key. That's why I haven't . . . Look out!"

Droopy pointed to the horizon where a 'sploder had peeked out from behind a rock formation and thrown a flaming container of explosives. Everyone scattered, and the explosives landed harmlessly in the middle of the group. A moment later it detonated with much sound and fury, but injured nobody.

The squad's weapons were in their hands in the blink of an eye. Mikaleh had the best angle, and unloaded on the 'sploder with her legendary assault rifle before the creature could duck back out of the way. It splattered everywhere, and tanks of unthrown explosive clattered to the ground by its feet. One of the tanks rolled across the landscape directly at Mikaleh. She stopped it with her foot like a soccer ball.

"Well, *that* one certainly wasn't out of range," Mikaleh said. "We'll have to be careful and watch for others going forward. Speaking of going forward, there's no question that we've entered Twine Peaks now . . . so where do we go from here? The Traveler made it sound like we ought to just look for the most forbidding, unpleasant place possible."

"That's going to be hard around here," Janet said. "There are so many good options."

"We'll have to take it bit by bit," Mikaleh said. "Look at the landscape in front of us—everything we see. If you were out for a stroll, where would you *not* want to go?"

The choices in front of them included a gradually narrowing path that led through 'sploder-infested hills, a sheer wall of rock, and a twisting trail off to one side that seemed to lead into a dark cave.

"I vote cave," said Sammy.

"Yes," agreed Sam. "Cave for me too. I know that there are 'sploders straight ahead, but it feels like there's going to be something *even worse* down in that cave."

"I'm with you," said Janet. "Plus, I bet it's all hot and gross down there."

"Good," said Mikaleh. "And what about you, Droopy?"

The husk merely shrugged.

"Okay," said Mikaleh. "The cave it is. Follow me, everyone. Just make sure to leave some space in case there are more ambushes. Which there probably will be . . ."

Heeding these words, the squad took turns heading for the dark obsidian cave. The interior of the cave was hot and smothering and it was hard to breathe.

"Yep," Janet quipped. "Definitely wouldn't choose to spend any more time in here than I had to."

"But look at the ground beneath our feet," Mikaleh said as they turned on their flashlights.

"There's a good deal of traffic here," said Sam. "Oh my. It looks like almost every kind of husk footprint."

"That's what I'm seeing too," said Mikaleh. "Quite a few husks come through here. What's forbidding to us might not be so forbidding to a husk."

"Exactly."

The squad looked up. It was Droopy who had spoken.

"Husks and humans seem to find different things gross," he said. "That's why I didn't have any good input before. Like, it feels totally pleasant in here to me. But before, when I was following you guys, and we were in that sunlit forest, and it was seventy-two degrees with a gentle breeze, and there was the smell of tree-ripened apples in the air . . . Yeah, that made me want to puke. But I think all of you actually liked it."

"You know, I think we *do* find different things pleasant and unpleasant," said Janet.

"So, as we go forward," Mikaleh said, stalking deeper into the cave, "when I ask the squad where they would *least* like to go, pretend I'm asking you what the *most* appealing path forward would be."

"Okay," said Droopy. "I can remember that. It'll actually be fun. Like some kind of reverse-game or something."

"Yes," Mikaleh said. "Or something."

They crept deeper into the forbidding cave.

"Hey," Sammy said as they approached a winding fissure that seemed to descend into utter blackness and stench. "This looks like a place I'd never, ever want to go. Droopy, your thoughts."

The husk carefully approached the forbidding black opening and sniffed.

"Aww, reminds me of home," he said.

"All right," Mikaleh said. "The scary fissure it is."

Ducking down, the squad crept into the terrifying blackness—a cave within a cave. The fissure was small and not every squad member could easily fit. Mikaleh thought to herself that the one advantage of this situation was that at least they could not be ambushed. Above and below, and to either side of them, was a rock wall far too thick for even a well-swung pickaxe to penetrate.

"It's kind of tight in here," said Sammy.

"It's *very* tight in here," Janet complained.

"Are you guys kidding?" said Droopy. "When the rock walls pinch in, just dislocate your shoulder blades and twist through like I do."

"But see, not being rotting corpse monsters, we're not able to do that so easily," Janet protested.

"Well, nobody's perfect," responded Droopy.

They walked deeper and deeper into the fissure. Just as the rock walls seemed as though they would tighten and tighten until they came together in a dead end, the fissure opened up. There was no larger cave beyond, but instead a small ledge in the side of a sheer cliff. There were several other rock cliffs above it. And below? There, the squad found a roiling sea of lava.

"Ahh," said Droopy, breathing in the lava fumes. "Smells like the soup my mother used to make. Wonderful!"

Mikaleh wondered if, technically speaking, husks needed to breathe. Maybe Droopy was just breathing in the lava fumes for fun.

"Well, this is an annoying dead end," Janet said, taking care to steady herself against the rock wall. "I guess that 'following your nose by heading toward the worst possible place' technique doesn't always work, eh?"

"I don't know about that," Mikaleh said. "Take a look in the distance there."

"What?" said Janet. "You mean that island of black rock set waaaaaaay out into the lava?"

Mikaleh nodded. "Take a look at the top of it," she said.

She pulled out a sniper scope, took a hard look through it, and then handed it to Janet with great satisfaction.

"You're right," said Janet, peering out across the lava. "Wow! There's a little fort there. Or something. Maybe a big fort. I can't quite make out all the details, even looking through this scope. But it's tall and square. Not a natural rock formation."

"If you're looking for a lava fortress around here, I can't think of anything that would be a better candidate," observed Sam.

"Yes," said Sammy. "I quite agree."

Though the terrible smell of the lava clearly intoxicated him, here it was Droopy who hesitated.

"We'll never make it, though," he told the group. "I like the odor of lava as much as the next husk, but I don't want it to melt me. Nobody could ever reach that island. A giant couldn't jump that far."

"We're not going to jump it," said Mikaleh. "We're going to build a bridge across the lava."

"Oh, *right!*" said Droopy. "Building things. Heh. I always forget about how humans can do that. I suppose it should preoccupy me more, because husks are always tearing down and attacking things that get built. As a husk, I'm used to thinking of building as something that the 'other side' does. You know. Not something the good guys do."

"You husks think *you're* the good guys?" Janet asked skeptically.

"From our point of view, we totally are," Droopy insisted.

"Look, this partnership is a little weird for everybody," said Mikaleh. "We don't need to be good guys or bad guys right now. We just need to reach the Last Survivor."

"Fine," said Droopy. "But I don't see how a bunch of weirdos who are always building things *on other people's property without permission* could think of themselves as good guys. But fine. You go ahead with that."

Something important occurred to Sam.

"If you come along with us across a bridge, do you think you can resist the urge to break it up?" Sam asked. "From what I've observed, the husks' hatred for construction is deeply innate."

"Eh, I think I can control myself," Droopy said. "It's true that we hate things you humans build. But it's also true that we hate drowning in the lava. And I think we hate that more."

"Let's hope so," said Mikaleh. "Now, who has building materials?"

The group pooled their inventories and took a look at all they had. When it was clear that everything had been accounted for, the faces of the squad were grim indeed.

"How did we not bring more building components?" Janet asked herself. "I mean, we have enough to build several houses or forts, but it's going to be a stretch to build a bridge that goes all the way across that lava."

"I wish this rock around us were mineable," said Sam, taking a couple of exploratory swings with a pickaxe, but producing only whitish-blue sparks. "No dice. It's totally impenetrable."

"Should we go back and look for more building materials?" Sammy asked.

Mikaleh looked over her shoulder, back into the dark reaches of the fissure.

"I don't know if it's worth it," she pronounced. "We've been lucky that, so far, the only challenge we've encountered here has been a few 'sploders. If we took the time to go all the way back to where we started, we might not be so lucky."

Sam carefully studied the pile of building materials and did some quick calculations in his notepad.

"Okaaaaay," he finally pronounced. "Given the distance to the island—which I can calculate using the length of the shadows around us and the height of the sun—it looks like we might have just enough building materials to build a bridge across the lava to the edge of the island."

"That's great," said Mikaleh.

Then Sam added: "But . . ."

Mikaleh rolled her eyes. "But *what*?" she pressed.

"But the bridge will have to be very thin," said Sam. "To reach the island, it can only be one plank wide. And we can't make any mistakes. Every piece will need to be used. No defects allowed."

"That shouldn't be a problem," said Mikaleh. "We can all get across a thin bridge if we walk single-file. And we've got the best builder in the world—Janet—in our squad. She can craft every piece of the bridge. I can't remember the last time Janet made a miscalculation or mistake."

"Okay," said Sam. "But then also . . ."

"What is it *now*?" Mikaleh pressed.

"Well, if that island is made of the same rock that this cliff is—which it certainly looks to be—then we won't be able to mine any new building materials while we're there," Sam explained.

"So?" said Mikaleh.

"So if anything happens to the bridge after we cross it . . . we're going to be stuck out there," Sam said ominously.

"Well then," Mikaleh said, "we'll just have to find the Last Survivor quickly, before anything can happen to the bridge. C'mon. We haven't a moment to lose."

Mikaleh spurred her squad into action. While Janet began building, the rest of the squad took turns feeding her wood, stone, and metal from their collective inventories.

"You're not hiding any building material in there between your ribs?" Sammy said to Droopy.

"Don't even joke about that," the husk said. "Humans have tried to build structures out of some very good friends of mine. It's something of a sore point in the husk community."

Janet built at a furious pace. Yet being the greatest constructor in the world meant that she could work quickly while still doing a quality job. Bit by bit, the bridge began extending out over the large lake of lava.

"Be careful you guys," Janet said as she worked. "Normally I'd put in guardrails for a build like this, but I guess I've got to save everything just for the floor of the bridge. One wrong move, and you could fall into the lava."

"Don't worry about us," Mikaleh said. "We're very careful people. You just stay focused on building the best bridge that you can."

They slowly made their way farther out across the lake of lava. When they were nearly halfway to the island, the details of the fortress came into focus. It was indeed an intentional construction, and it was immense.

"I wonder if they built that whole thing just to keep the Last Survivor in," wondered Sammy. "Maybe he was so powerful that they needed to. Or maybe they just wanted to throw him in the scariest place that already existed. Maybe it had already been built years before by humans. Either way, yikes."

"Yeah," agreed Mikaleh. "It's not a place where I'd choose to spend more time than I had to. All the more reason to get in and get out as fast as we can."

Suddenly, there was an unexpected and tre-mendous explosion a few feet to the side of the half-built bridge. It was so unexpected that Janet lost her balance and wobbled. Sam and Sammy had to grab each of her flailing arms and pull—hard!—to keep her from falling into the lava.

"What was that?" Janet said when she recov-ered. "Lava doesn't just explode."

The squad looked around nervously. Then a voice cried out: "Hey! Up here!"

The squad looked up.

High on the edges of the sheer rock cliffs sur-rounding the lake of lava stood a menacing collec-tion of 'sploders. They all shouldered explosives.

"That was a warning shot!" one of them declared.

The quad hesitated. Normally, even a large group of 'sploders would be no problem for Mikaleh and her colleagues. But nothing about this situation was normal. Not only did the 'sploders have the high ground, but only one of their tanks could demolish the bridge. Because Janet—like all master constructors—favored a cantilevered approach to building that meant that every piece of the bridge was depending on the one behind it. All the 'sploders needed to do was knock a single piece of the bridge away, and the entire thing would fall into the lava.

Mikaleh realized that their situation was very precarious indeed.

The 'sploders, it was immediately clear, also sensed that they had the upper hand.

"Let him go!" one of the 'sploders said.

"Yes," said another. "Or we'll break your bridge and send you all falling into the lava."

Janet and Mikaleh looked at each other.

"They think you're our prisoner, Droopy," Janet whispered out of the corner of her mouth.

Mikaleh tried to think.

"But if you send us falling into the lava, then won't he fall in as well?" she shouted back up at the 'sploders.

The creatures seemed to consider this for a moment.

"Yes," they eventually said. "But you would fall in too, which would be the main thing."

The 'sploders all nodded at one another in agreement on this point.

Suddenly, Droopy himself spoke up.

"Thank you guys," Droopy said to the 'sploders. "I really appreciate the backup. I certainly do. Really feels good to know you're there for me. But I've got this. These prisoners are going to get out to the fortress just fine."

The 'sploders lowered their explosives and looked at one another.

"They are . . . *your* prisoners?" one of the 'sploders asked doubtfully.

"Yes!" Droopy announced brightly. "They're totally, um, captured by me right now."

"Because that squad looks really tough," one 'sploder said.

"Yes," added another. "And it looks like they've got all kinds of weapons on them that would be really good for fighting husks and mist monsters."

"No, they're . . . not all that tough," Droopy said, trying to sound like he was telling the truth. "They're actually quite wimpy. And I'm very, *very* tough, so it works out."

"Not to be rude, but you kind of just look like a regular husk," said one of the 'sploders.

"Yeah," said another. "A regular husk whose neck and spine are even weirder than you usually see."

"That . . . uh . . . is just another one of my awesome powers," Droopy said, clearly grasping for explanations.

"And you're taking the humans to the fortress in the lava?" another 'sploder said with increasing skepticism.

"Oh, yes," said Droopy.

"I thought only the Last Survivor was kept there," a 'sploder said.

"This is a new policy," Droopy said.

"Well, I've never heard of it," said a 'sploder.

"This is Twine Peaks though," said Droopy. "We're from Stonewood, and this is a Stonewood policy. They roll all the rule changes out in Stonewood first."

"I never heard that," the 'sploder said. "This all seems rather strange."

The 'sploders fingered the giant explosives on their shoulders. The squad could hear their fat fingers drumming noisily against the tanks. They were clearly still itching to send them all into the lava.

But Droopy remained brave and stuck to his script.

"Now if you'll excuse me, I have to get these prisoners to the lava fortress on time or I'll get in trouble," he said. "Continue building the bridge—servant!—or I'll beat you up again."

"Um, right away," Janet said, playing along.

She began to create new pieces of the bridge.

"That's right away, *sir*!" Droopy snarled at her.

Mikaleh had never heard Droopy snarl before. It was quite convincing. Perhaps all husks had some innate grumpiness inside them.

"Right away, *sir*!" said Janet, giving Droopy a wink.

For a moment, the squad was silent as Janet built more extensions into the bridge. Above them, the 'sploders were conferring. This was the first time that most of the squad had heard 'sploders speaking, so their tone of voice was not something for which they had much reference. But it seemed to them that the 'sploders were not entirely buying it.

Eventually, one of the 'sploders called down to Droopy.

"Look, we aren't sure we believe you. We've never seen a husk escorting prisoners to the lava fortress before, and it doesn't look like this squad is weak enough for you to handle them yourself. We're going to blow them into the lava just to be on the safe side. You can get out of the way—or not—but don't say we didn't warn you."

"Uh . . . Uh . . . don't do that," Droopy called to the 'sploders. "You shouldn't do that because . . . because . . ."

Mikaleh could see on Droopy's face that the husk was out of ideas. At the same time—even though Janet was building onto the end of the bridge with all her might—they were still a good distance out from the island. If the 'sploders threw their bombs now, there was no chance Mikaleh could see of escaping their fates at the bottom of a lava-filled lake.

"Come on, guys!" Mikaleh shouted in an exaggerated voice. She gave Droopy a wink and a smile that said "Play along."

"This super-powerful husk is distracted talking to the 'sploders!" she continued. "Now's our chance to overpower him and escape."

Mikaleh stood up straight and ran right at Droopy.

For an instant, Droopy's jaw dropped and his eyes bulged, as though he did not know what to do (or even what was happening). Then Mikaleh, in the midst of her sprint, glanced down at Droopy's fist.

Droopy raised his arm as if to say "You mean this?"

In the same moment, Mikaleh ran full-tilt into it. She jerked back as though she had hit a brick wall. Then she spun around twice and face-planted into the floor of the bridge. It was very dramatic.

A collective: "Ooooh!" went up from the 'sploders, and some unshouldered their explosives.

"I'll show that husk who's boss," Sammy cried, drawing one of his swords. "And I'll bet that *he doesn't even remember any of his cool karate moves anymore.*"

Sammy said this last part so loudly that Droopy immediately got the idea.

As Sammy and Droopy faced off, Sammy began swinging his sword while Droopy dropped back into a martial arts stance. With every swing, Sammy seemed to chop the air where the husk had been standing only a moment before. Droopy appeared to be a master of evasion. Then Droopy did a karate chop. It was pretty gentle as karate chops go, but when his rotting hand brushed the side of Sammy's blade, Sammy sent the sword flinging dramatically out of his grip, high above their heads, and into the bubbling lava below.

"Oh no," Sammy cried. "He's disarmed me! Not another karate chop! Please, mister husk."

Droopy's eyes narrowed as he smiled.

"Call me *sir*!" Droopy commanded, and landed another glancing blow against Sammy's solar plexus. Using his ninja double-jump skills, Sammy turned several backward somersaults as if reeling with the force of Droopy's hand. He twisted through the air and landed next to Janet, just an inch from the lava's edge.

"Wow!" one of the 'sploders cried. There was a smattering of applause from the ledges.

"You'll never defeat me!" Sam said, stepping up. "My awesome psychic brainpower has been enough to flummox even the cleverest of husks."

"But we aren't really known for being clever," Droopy whispered.

"Just play along," Sam whispered back.

Sam closed his eyes and put one finger to his temple, as if he was thinking very hard. Then with his other hand, he pointed two fingers at Droopy. He screwed up his face until his temples bulged, and made an odd humming noise. To Droopy, he looked like someone casting a spell.

Droopy shrugged and began doing the same thing. He closed his eyes, pointed his finger at Sam, and made vibrating sounds.

Up on the cliffs above, the 'sploders looked at one another. They had clearly never seen anything like this before. Though they might have been confused, it was clear they were also entertained. They had seen squads exploded into lava before by their bombs. But this was a whole new ballgame.

As the 'sploders watched in awe and confusion, the expression on Sam's face became more and more strained. He began to frown. He breathed hard, as if he had just been running a sprint. Then, gradually, he started to lower himself, as though a giant weight were being placed on his shoulders.

"No . . ." Sam said, as if very frustrated. "I can't believe it. My psychic weaponry has never . . . been . . . defeated!"

And with that, Sam collapsed to the floor of the bridge. He was defeated, but clearly still alive. He kicked his leg intermittently, like a dog.

Droopy raised his hands above his head in triumph.

Though they were not sure what they had just seen, the 'sploders gave it a thunderous round of applause. There were many "oohs" and "aahs" is if Droopy were a magician who had just performed an astounding feat.

"Sorry for attacking you . . . *sir*," Sam said as he slunk back to his side of the bridge.

"What about you?" Droopy asked, looking to Janet. "Do you want to try your luck?"

"No way," said Janet, still building furiously. "I'm just a constructor. You've already beaten the toughest warriors in our band. Even if I built a metal building all around you, I'm sure you'd just knock it down a second later."

"That's true," Droopy declared. "I totally would."

Even though his arm muscles were old and green and rotting, Droopy flexed them to indicate how powerful he was feeling.

Then a voice up above said: "Uh, so . . . never mind, I guess."

Droopy glanced up to the 'sploder who was speaking.

"It . . . It looks like you know what you're doing."

"Yeah," said one 'sploder to another. "It also looks like if we disobeyed him, he could come kick our butts!"

"Yes," the first 'sploder said. "So please just carry on with your mission down there. And if you ever need any help from us, just come let us know. We guard these cliffs."

"Thank you," Droopy said, cracking his knuckles.

As the "defeated" squad remained on their backs, Janet continued to craft. One by one, the 'sploders above them gradually slunk away. And all the while, Janet continued to build like the wind. After a few minutes, Mikaleh felt comfortable standing up.

"It's okay, guys," she said. "I think they're gone."

Sam and Sammy rose to their feet.

"That was exciting," Sammy said, brushing himself off. "I had no idea we were all such good actors. We should put on plays or something."

"I'm too shy to be a real actor," said Sam. "I can only act in front of audiences of husks and mist monsters. They're much more gentle critics. And if they don't like your acting, you can just shoot them."

"I think we all owe some thanks to Droopy for his quick thinking and willingness to play along," said Mikaleh.

"Yeah, nice work," Janet said as she continued to build. "And I don't just mean nice work 'for a husk.' I mean nice work for anybody, period."

"It's been awhile since anybody got the drop on our squad," Mikaleh continued. "Ages, really. Thank goodness you were there to help with that."

"No problem," Droopy said. "I feel like you guys did the bulk of the work. Mostly I just pretended to know karate and be a psychic and stuff."

"You'd be surprised how many people wouldn't be able to do even that much," Mikaleh said with a grin.

With the 'sploders out of the way, the squad had nothing to do but watch as Janet crafted the long, thin bridge the rest of the way to the shore of the island that held the fortress. The island was very close now. Mikaleh could see a large, central doorway, and several barred windows. The fortress had a crenulated top like a castle. Light seemed to come from within, but Mikaleh couldn't tell if it was from torches burning on the walls, or only the reflected glow from the lake of lava that surrounded it.

As they neared the beach of the island, Janet seemed to slow her building. Then she stopped.

"Uh-oh," she said.

"Uh-oh?" said Mikaleh. "What does that mean?"

"It's not a *big* uh-oh," Janet clarified. "Just a little one. There aren't quite enough building components to reach the beach."

"Maybe my math was off," said Sam. "I always forget to carry the two in tense situations."

"It just means we'll have to jump," Janet said. "Not too far. I think all of us should be able to make it easy. We're pretty good jumpers, and, of course, Sammy's amazing."

Then, behind them, a strange gurgling noise arose. Mikaleh slowly realized that this was Droopy clearing his throat.

"So . . . about that," Droopy said. "Husks can't really jump, per se. Have you noticed how when we're attacking you, you can build little half-walls that are just knee-high, and we *still* have to stop and claw through them? That's because of the not-being-able-to-jump so much."

"Huh," said Mikaleh. "So what are we going to do?"

"One of us could jump to the island and look for materials we could use to craft the rest of the bridge," Sammy suggested. "Though I don't see anything right now that appears useful. It's all sand and black obsidian rock that would break your pickaxe."

"Don't overthink this," Droopy suggested. "You can just throw me."

"What?" the rest of the squad said more or less in unison.

"Sure," said the husk. "Think about it. Most of my insides have rotted away, and I don't really have any blood. Most creatures are like ninety percent water anyhow. I don't have any of that stuff. That's what 'husk' means. Just an outer shell."

Sam said: "You know, he's right. May I?"

He gestured to the husk.

"But of course," Droopy replied.

Sam reached into where Droopy's belly should have been, gripped him around the spine, and picked him up.

"Wow!" Sam said. "It's like lifting a hat rack. He weighs almost nothing at all."

"Yes," Droopy said. "I think I could also make myself very aerodynamic in terms of flight. My only concern is that that sand on the beach looks pretty thin. I'd hate to break my skull and bones against the rock."

"We'll make sure that doesn't happen," Mikaleh said. "Janet, build the rest of the bridge, even if it doesn't quite reach the island. We've come too far to go back now."

"Aye aye!" Janet said enthusiastically, and quickly crafted the final lengths of bridge into place.

It almost reached the beach. A good running start, and any of the squad members would be safe leaping over the lava.

"Okay," said Janet. "I should go first. Even though my hands are tired from all that building, I'm still the best person here at catching things. I was a catcher on my high school softball team. And I don't think Droopy weighs *that* much more than a softball."

"Sounds good to me," said Mikaleh. "The rest of us will be throwers. Droopy, lie down."

While Janet easily made the leap from the end of the bridge onto dry land, Droopy got down on his back and lay flat. Mikaleh grabbed his arms, and Sam and Sammy each took one of his legs.

"Wow," said Sammy. "This guy weighs nothing."

"I know, right?" said Sam.

"Okay," Mikaleh said. "Is everybody ready?"

"I'm as ready as I'll ever be," said Droopy.

The rest of the squad nodded.

"Okay," said Mikaleh, beginning to swing Droopy's bony arms. "Here we go. One . . . two . . . *three!*"

And with these words, they sent Droopy flying out across the lava. As he flew, Droopy raised his arms, as if doing a bad imitation of a bird. Mikaleh realized that he was trying to use his clothing to catch the wind, like a sail. It didn't look as though it was making him fly any farther, but Mikaleh liked the idea that Droopy could feel as though he was helping.

"Wheeee!" Droopy cried as he flew through the air.

A few tense seconds later, he landed safely in Janet's arms. She carefully placed him on the beach.

"Yep," Janet said. "Just like a softball."

The rest of the squad leapt down from the bridge and joined Janet and Droopy on the island's small beach. Ahead of them, the entrance to the fortress loomed, high and wide. Large metal doors sealed it shut. (Would they break under the force of a pickaxe? That would have to be tested shortly, Mikaleh realized.)

As the squad began making tentative explorations of the fortress exterior, Sam motioned Mikaleh over and the two spoke privately.

"Hey," Sam told her. "So what I was saying before about a test to find out if we could trust Droopy? Anyhow, I couldn't have come up with anything better than what we just experienced. Droopy put himself on the line with those 'sploders. He had the opportunity to betray us and leave us stranded out there in the lava, but he didn't do that. And then to top it off, he literally put his life in our hands when he trusted us to throw him onto the island. I don't think there's anything he could have done, frankly, to make himself more trustworthy."

"You know, I believe I feel the same way," said Mikaleh.

Yet even as these words were out of her mouth, Mikaleh wondered if the dangers they still had to face would change this. She looked up at the forbidding walls of the fortress and thought about the mysterious Last Survivor imprisoned within. Mikaleh knew that there were perhaps no bonds stronger than those between brothers or sisters. Would things change when they finally stood in the presence of Droopy's brother once more?

Mikaleh was not sure if she knew. For the moment, however, Droopy had proved trustable. Mikaleh would let that be enough.

CHAPTER ELEVEN

S o, there's been a lot of talk so far on this journey about things 'feeling like traps' or 'looking like traps' and so on . . . but you gotta admit. *This feels a lot like a trap.*"

No one disagreed with Janet. They had ventured a little farther away from the lava, and now stood before the impressive metal door at the front of the fortress. They had searched it carefully, inspecting every edge—looking for keyholes and tapping it with a pickaxe to see if it felt breakable—when Janet saw something that nobody else had observed. The door was, very slightly, ajar.

"I mean, you wouldn't build a door this high and big and strong . . . and then just *not close it,*" said Janet. "Or would you?"

"It is very odd," said Sam. "Perhaps they've never had to close it because nobody has ever gotten close enough to enter it before. Maybe no one ever built a bridge across that lava like we did."

"Droopy, how long did you say your brother has been locked up here?" asked Mikaleh.

"Oh, you know," the husk replied. "Since the earliest days of the Storm. So quite a long time."

Mikaleh knew that in large organizations, people often forgot about places and things that were not being used every day. Mikaleh did not know precisely how the husk leadership worked, but she began to think they might have assumed the Last Survivor was locked up so well that they could stop checking on him.

"I agree that it could be a trap," Mikaleh said. "But I also know how bad people can be about forgetting to lock up. Let's give it a go and see what there is to see."

Mikaleh took a deep breath and pressed hard against the heavy metal door. The giant hinges on which it rested were old and rusty, and they squeaked loudly. By the time Mikaleh had the door pushed wide enough for a human (or a husk) to fit through, half her squad had their fingers in their ears.

Mikaleh took her hands off the door. The loud screeching stopped.

"Well," Sam said, taking his fingers from his ears. "If they didn't know we were coming before, they probably know now."

Mikaleh was annoyed at having announced their presence through the shrieking door, but was also relieved. No traps or bombs had gone off. The door had not been electrified. And nothing had attacked them.

Then, just as Mikaleh began to lean forward to peer into the shadowy hallway beyond the door, a very deep, very loud voice said: "Who's there?"

Mikaleh withdrew her head for a moment. She looked at her squad and brought a single finger up to her lips. They nodded and stayed quiet.

"Hello?" the deep voice continued. "Who is there?"

"What the heck is that?" Sammy whispered.

"I don't know," said Janet. "But it's going to be enormous."

Mikaleh shushed the both of them. Then she turned on a flashlight and shined it into the tunnel beyond. At first she saw nothing. Rocky black tunnel wall. The interior was dimly lit by torches set into the walls. She shined her light down the hallway. The corridor terminated in another huge door with a flywheel like a bank vault. To one side of the door was a small concrete stand that looked much like an outdoor birdbath. Atop it were a pair of very small reflective eyes. The rest was concealed in the darkness.

"I'm going in," said Mikaleh, taking her assault rifle out of her inventory and stepping into the corridor.

The rest of the squad followed.

"HELLO!" the voice boomed again, so loud it made Mikaleh jump. "Who is coming? Now I hear footsteps."

Mikaleh remained silent. The sound seemed to come from the end of the hall. She saw nothing large enough to have so commanding a voice.

Halfway down the hall, the small creature atop the stone platform came into view. It was about the size of a small dog and looked very much like a piranha with one heck of an underbite. Beneath its large head was a tiny body. It had long, spindly limbs.

The voice came again, and this time, Mikaleh saw the tiny creature's long jaw move in time with the words.

"Seriously," it said. "Look, I *know* you're there."

"What on earth?" Mikaleh said, despite herself.

"Aha!" it said, sounding very proud of itself. "See? I knew you were there!"

"What is that?" asked Sammy.

"It's a troll," Sam informed him. "You don't see them too frequently, at least not outside of the Whack-a-Troll game. Sometimes I see them in abandoned buildings, just kind of floating like ghosts. They're very mysterious."

"Who else is there?" the troll demanded. "Who is it who knows so much about trolls?"

Mikaleh sniffed the air as if detecting something amiss. Then she took a few more silent steps closer to the troll. It remained seated where it was, very much like a bird in its birdbath.

"You're not able to see," Mikaleh said.

"Of course I can't see," the troll boomed. "If I could, would I have to ask so many questions? Yet, that's a fair point, I suppose," the troll said.

"Why is your voice so deep?" Mikaleh asked.

And here, the troll did not respond immediately, but rather laughed so hard that its tiny belly shook. When it had recovered, it said: "Perhaps I must take back what I just said about you knowing so much about us."

"Why?" Mikaleh said.

"Because, *for a troll*, my voice is exceedingly high," it said. "Most trolls have voices that are so low, humans cannot actually hear them. Or, when they do hear them, they mistake troll speech for a tugboat horn, or a bass guitar, or an undersea earthquake."

"Wow," said Mikaleh. "Those sounds are pretty deep."

The tiny troll nodded.

"My nickname with other trolls is actually 'Squeaky' because my voice is so odd and high," it said. "You would not believe the teasing I endured as a child."

"I'm sorry you were teased," Mikaleh said. "That's not nice."

"Perhaps it was better that I could not see the faces of my tormentors," said the troll.

"Yikes," Sammy chimed. "Squeaky-voiced and blind? That must have been challenging."

"I, like all trolls, am born to persevere," the troll said proudly. "And also to haunt and annoy humans whenever possible. Because that's really fun!"

"I see," Mikaleh said. "Say, now that we're friends and all, can I ask what you know about this enormous door?"

"You mean the one behind me with the big circular handle?" it asked.

"Yes," said Mikaleh.

"Well, of course I know about that," said the troll. "I'm the one stationed here to guard it. By the way, it's not open is it?"

"No," Mikaleh began. "It's not op—"

The troll cut her off with peals of thunderous laughter.

"Hahahaha! I know it's not open. I'm just messing with you."

"Very funny," said Mikaleh.

"I know it's not open because I'm the only one who knows how it's opened," the troll continued. "There's a trick to it, y'see."

"A trick?" said Mikaleh.

"That only *I* know," confirmed the troll.

Suddenly, Janet stepped closer.

"Not to be nosy," said Janet. "But why would anybody leave a tiny, blind troll to guard such a big important door?"

"First of all, I'm medium-sized for a troll," the troll said. "Second of all, the biggest security problem in a prison is always impersonation. Ask anybody. So what I do is take that out of the equation."

"Explain what you mean," said Mikaleh.

"Well," said the troll. "Suppose that you're somebody who wants to pretend to be someone with access to this fortress. In most situations, if you're trying to sneak in past a guard, what are you going to do? I'll tell you what. You're going to dress up as somebody who works there. Or you're going to forge somebody's badge or pass or security ID."

"Ahh!" Sam said. "But none of that will work on you because you can't see."

"Now you're getting it," said the troll. "They say that when you're blind, the other senses get stronger. I don't know if that's true, but I know the senses I do have are very good. I have other ways of telling if someone is qualified to pass through or not."

"This is fascinating," said Sam. "I never thought of having a system like that, but it does make a kind of sense."

The troll smiled through its long, jagged teeth, obviously appreciative of the compliment.

"For example," the troll continued. "The reason I haven't pressed a button on my podium—the one that summons guards and floods the floor with lava and all kind of nasty things—is the way that you smell."

The squad looked at one another. Janet discreetly sniffed at her armpit.

"Now, it's not because you smell either good or bad," said the troll. "It's because you sort of smell . . . like the Last Survivor. That tells me that something's up. That even though I have not encountered you before, you may have a legitimate reason to be here. That there's more to the story. Which is, again, the thing stopping me from immediately flipping my switch."

Mikaleh took Droopy aside. She didn't need to say anything. Droopy understood.

"I probably do smell a lot like my brother," Droopy whispered, nodding. "We're practically twins. Literally twins, I should say. Like, we were born at the same time, and we're identical. Did I mention that? He even has a neck like mine. But if you were to call the Last Survivor 'Droopy' it might end very badly for you. I, on the other hand, have learned to accept it, haven't I?"

"What's that?" said the troll, sniffing the air. "What are you whispering? Speak up!"

Mikaleh had an idea. She strode back over to where the troll sat on his birdbath podium.

"So, this is a bit embarrassing," Mikaleh said. "We're trying to keep it secret, as a matter of national security, you see? But the Last Survivor escaped, and we had to capture him again."

"What!?" said the troll, its deep voice booming. Its unseeing eyes rolled manically in alarm.

"Sssshhh," Mikaleh shushed him. "It's all right now because we've caught him."

"Is he here now?" the troll said, growing increasingly nervous. "Is that what I smell? I thought I was smelling his residue on you."

"No, it's actually him," said Mikaleh. "And we need to get him back inside his cell before anyone knows he got out. Of course, after that, we'll need to do a complete security review."

"Is my job safe, d'you think?" the troll asked. "I don't know what I'd do with myself if I wasn't a security guard on an island surrounded by lava. Once you've done this for a living for a while, everything else sounds dull in comparison."

"Don't worry," said Mikaleh. "He, uh, escaped some other way. But we've got the gold key with the special red handle, so his powers are limited. He's actually quite harmless. Here. Why don't you inspect him just to make certain we're telling you the truth?"

Mikaleh gestured to Janet, who was standing beside Droopy. She shoved his shoulder, pushing him forward. Droopy stared back at Janet in annoyance. Janet pursed her lips and pointed insistently to the tiny troll. Droopy loped over.

When Droopy arrived at the little platform, the troll began to sniff him. Droopy's face said that he thought this was a little weird, but he still allowed the inspection.

"My goodness," said the troll. "Yes, I think this smells just like him. It's been so long since I was in the same room as the Last Survivor. But my nose usually doesn't lie. Let me do one more test."

The troll extended its disturbingly long, thin arms and began to paw at Droopy's breastbone. The troll gently lifted the rags that composed Droopy's clothing. He felt the texture of Droopy's knucklebones. The expression on the troll's face said that he might have been a chef sampling an exquisite broth.

"Ahh, yes," said the troll. "The Last Survivor indeed! With my hands, I can feel things that no impostor could ever have built into a disguise or costume, no matter how skilled. The Last Survivor was born with a strange indentation on the middle knuckle of his right hand, for example. Nobody knows about it."

"Yes," said Mikaleh. "I'm sure we've got our man."

"But why does he not speak?" said the troll. "In all of my times being in the same room as the Last Survivor, this is the longest he's been quiet. Usually, he's all 'Why are you jerks doing this?' and 'Why don't you let me go?' and so forth. It's very annoying."

"We, uh . . . uh . . ." Mikaleh began.

Then she took a handkerchief she used for polishing the barrel of her assault rifle (and sometimes for wiping her nose) out of her back right pocket. She looked at Droopy urgently and opened her mouth like she was at the dentist. Droopy did not quite understand what this meant, but he opened his mouth in the same way. (Maybe Mikaleh was telling him he had something stuck in his teeth?)

And then, in a quick, violent motion, Mikaleh stuffed the handkerchief into his mouth. Droopy's eyes rolled and his expression asked *What are you doing?*

"Eww," Sam whispered quietly. "I've seen her wipe her nose with that thing."

"Uh," Mikaleh said loudly. "The Last Survivor can't talk because we've put a rag in his mouth."

Immediately, the troll's long arms went to Droopy's mouth, verifying that this was true.

"We don't know if his powers are linked to casting spells somehow," Mikaleh continued, "and we don't want to take a chance. Plus, we don't want him to be able to call for help. And on top of that, it's punishment for being a bad Last Survivor and trying to escape."

"He has indeed been very bad, it seems," said the troll. "Very, very bad. All right then. Thank goodness you were able to catch and return him, whoever you good souls are. We are thankful for you."

"It's no problem," said Mikaleh.

"Now if you'll just give me the password, I can go ahead and open up that door for you," it said.

Mikaleh's stomach fell. Janet smacked her own forehead. Droopy's jaw fell so low that the rag came halfway out of his mouth.

"Just kidding!!!" the troll said with a laugh. "There's no password. I just like doing that to people. It can be a little too quiet around here. I have to find ways of amusing myself where I can."

"No problem," said Mikaleh as she tried to relax once more.

"I'll just press another little button on the console in front of me here," said the troll. "Boom! There you go."

No sooner were these words out of the tiny troll's mouth than there was a loud grating sound. The flywheel on the vault-like door began to turn by itself, and it opened wide. Beyond it was another hallway lit by torches. This hallway was like a ramp leading down. Mikaleh could not see the end of it.

"Thank you," Mikaleh said. The squad and Droopy began making their way down the mysterious ramp.

"No problem," said the troll as they passed. "And thank *you* for recapturing the Last Survivor.

Plus, while I'm thinking of it, I don't think any of the other traps have been disabled. But I'm sure they told you what to do. Okay, see you later."

Suddenly, the great vault-like door began closing behind them. The squad exchanged a worried glance, and then a thunderous sound shook the walls as the vault slammed shut.

"Wait," said Janet. "Did that troll just say something about traps?"

"That's what I heard too," said Mikaleh.

"Could he have been joking?" Janet asked.

"The troll sounded serious to me," said Mikaleh. "Polite, but serious. I definitely don't think he was kidding."

"What kind of traps would they even need?" said Sammy. "I mean, nobody could get past that door."

"*We* just did," Sam pointed out.

"Yes, we're very smart," said Sammy. "We know how to use tricks. Plus, we had Droopy. Which was a pretty lucky thing, now that I think about it."

"Well," Sam said thoughtfully. "Maybe the traps are there to test other things. If the door stops one kind of intruder, perhaps the traps are designed to stop another."

There was an awkward pause. The squad began examining the walls, ceiling, and floor of the sloping corridor where they stood—and each sconce set into the wall.

Then Mikaleh said: "C'mon, guys. We can do this. We need to be careful, but not paranoid! We're the best squad around. How many traps have we avoided or defused in the past?"

"Um, lots and lots of them," Sammy said.

"But they were mostly things like floor damage traps," Sam said.

"Yes," said Mikaleh. "There's nothing to be bashful about when it comes to floor traps. They pack a punch."

"I suppose," said Sam.

Her squad did not sound very convinced. Mikaleh realized she might have to lead the way to encourage them. She began heading farther down the sloping corridor.

"We've come this far," she said. "And we're very close. I'm not going to let some troll mumbling about traps scare me away from reaching the Last Survivor. Are you?"

The squad all mumbled some version of the fact that they supposed not. Then they all got in line and followed Mikaleh down the hallway to the unknown depths beyond.

CHAPTER TWELVE

Now we're talking!" said Janet.

"Wow," added Sammy. "It's sort of a relief! No, I'm serious. After going for so long wondering if something would be an elaborate trap setup, it's like a load off my mind to say 'This is definitely a trap!'"

"Yep," said Sam.

"But if you think about it, the troll was a little bit like a trap," said Sammy. "It felt like it to me anyway. It was trap-ish."

The rest of the squad looked at Sammy and shook their heads.

"What?" he said. "That's how it felt to me. And I have a right to my feelings."

Mikaleh cleared her throat.

"So fellas?" she said. "Maybe now we should figure out what we're actually going to do about this."

"Oh," Sammy said. "Oh yeah. This . . ."

The long, torch-lined ramp had taken them far beneath the island's surface. Down, down, down it had gone, seemingly to the bowels of the island. Just when Mikaleh had thought it could not possibly go on any longer, it had terminated in a large wide room with strange mosaic tiles spread across the floor. But what had captured Mikaleh's attention was not the floor of the room so much as the walls. This was because the walls were covered with RPGs of every sort. There were regular rocket launchers with angry faces painted on them, epic purple missile launchers, and legendary orange bazookas. And all of them were pointed outward, at all different parts of the room. It was hard for Mikaleh to guess which RPG might shoot where. There had to be hundreds of them.

Far across the room, on the other side of the tiles, was a single open doorway.

"Well, we know where we have to get to," said Janet, eyeing the doorway. "And we know that if we do something wrong, some of these RPGs are bound to shoot. Maybe all of them. But what makes them shoot? It must have something to do with these tiles on the floor."

The room was not well lit, but the squad could see that each tile was barely big enough for someone to stand on. And each one seemed to have a crude figure etched into it.

"I can't see well in this torchlight," Sam said, getting out his flashlight. "I want to get down closer and look at these things."

"Fine," said Mikaleh. "Just don't touch any of them."

"I'm not an idiot," said Sam.

Sam crept to the edge of the tiles and squatted down. He shined his light carefully across the face of the nearest tile. Then he surveyed the next one. And then the one after that.

Then he stood up again.

"They're husks," he pronounced.

"What?" said Mikaleh, taking out her own flashlight.

"Oh yeah," said Sammy, turning his head to the side. "Now I kind of see it too."

One by one, the members of the squad began to see the pattern in the tiles. They all fell into place at once, like the effect of an optical illusion or a magic eye painting.

"I see what you mean," said Mikaleh. "They're kind of painted abstractly but you can definitely see it. These tiles are meant to be regular husks. These are huskies. Then those with the arms extended are pitchers. The ones with their arms extended wearing dresses are lobbers. And the ones with beehives on their heads are, I'm guessing, beehives."

"You're right!" said Janet. "Why, every kind of husk on the planet has to be here."

"Yes," said Sam. "And it looks like some of the patterns repeat. There's a husky over there. And then, see, another one a few tiles over. And then another one a couple of tiles past that."

"Crazy," said Sammy. "Do you think it makes some sort of pattern? Or are they just randomly thrown together? I can remember putting down tile in my house in the days before the Storm. I always hated it when there was a pattern because it was so easy for me to mess it up."

"I don't know if there's a pattern," said Sam. "It kind of looks random to me at the moment."

"But these tiles . . ." Janet began. "They've got to be connected to the RPGs right? Like if you step on the wrong tile, you get an RPG launched at you?"

"That'd be my guess," Sam said.

"Ahh," said Janet. "Well, good thing I can just build us a bridge right over them . . . *except we used all our building components to build the bridge getting out here.*"

Mikaleh could tell that Janet was kind of angry about this situation. She expected Janet felt a bit naked as a constructor without any building materials. Like how a soldier might feel without any bullets. Suffice to say, Mikaleh certainly understood.

The squad put on their collective thinking cap and tried to puzzle a way forward.

"None of us can jump across, right?" Janet asked.

"Not even me," said Sammy. "It's three or four times farther than my best jump."

"Maybe we could throw Droopy, like we did before," Janet suggested.

"That would be a pretty long throw, though . . ." Sammy said hesitantly.

"Yes," said Mikaleh. "And then what good would it do us? He's on the other side, and we're over here."

"Well then he could . . . he could . . ." Janet stammered. "I don't know. It would be something anyway."

"Yes," said Mikaleh. "I suppose it would."

"I actually have an idea," said Droopy. "And it *doesn't* involve throwing me all the way across the room."

"Okay," said Mikaleh. "Shoot. Remember, in brainstorming there are no wrong answers."

"Oh," said Droopy. "I don't know if I actually have a brain to brainstorm with. For a lot of us husks, our heads are just hollow. So maybe

I'm just skull-storming. Anyhow, you're out of building material, but you're certainly not out of ammo. Why don't we throw a couple of grenades at the RPGs on the walls? I bet that would make 'em all explode at once. Kaboom! And the RPGs can't shoot at us if they're all exploded."

"Okay, two things," Sam said, approaching Droopy. "One—if we set off all these RPGs at once, it's probably going to kill us. It would create one massive explosion. It would probably send fire shooting all the way up the tunnel we just came from. We'd almost definitely be burned up. And two—assuming we survive that part, it would be deafeningly loud. Any thoughts we might have had of rescuing the Last Survivor would probably be gone for good; every creature in this fortress would immediately descend on us."

"Well . . . I mean . . . Okay . . ." said Droopy. "But it would still look pretty cool."

Sam smiled.

"You've got a point there," Sam said. "Right before it exploded all of us, it would almost certainly look pretty cool."

Droopy smiled in evident satisfaction that his point had been acknowledged.

"This is pretty good brainstorming," said Mikaleh. "But we're not quite there yet. Something tells me we're going to have to figure out how the tiles on the floor figure in."

"Darn it," said Janet. "This is going to be like one of those boring games I'm not very good at. Like crossword puzzles or sudoku."

Mikaleh smiled. "Looking for patterns doesn't have to be hard," she said. "I bet something in the images on the tiles will tell us which ones we can walk across without triggering the RPGs."

"I don't mean to boast," said Sam, "but unlike Janet, I am very good at spotting patterns."

"That's true; he is," agreed Sammy.

"Doing an initial survey of how frequently the blocks recur, I don't see anything," Sam said, gazing out across the tiles. "However, I wonder if it might have something to do with going from husk to husk. For example, maybe the pattern is weakest-to-strongest. So say you first step on a tile with a dwarf on it—you know, one of those little half-husks? Then you jump to a regular husk. Then to a husky. Then to a pitcher. Then to a 'sploder. Then to a beehive. And so on."

"Waaaait," said Janet. "I see what you mean, but isn't a 'sploder stronger than a beehive? Like, a more formidable foe?"

"I think it depends on the situation," Sammy offered. "I can definitely think of situations where I'd rather be fighting 'sploders, and I can think of situations where I'd rather be fighting beehives. Terrain. Time of day. How tired my sword-arm is feeling. These are all things that can impact my choice."

Mikaleh said: "I like the way you're thinking, Sam. I'll bet it does have something to do with the different tiles connecting like that. But how do we know it doesn't run the other way?"

"What do you mean 'the other way'?" said Sam.

"What if you're supposed to step on them strongest-to-weakest instead of weakest-to-strongest?" Mikaleh asked.

"Huh?" said Sam. "So you mean start with a zapper?"

"Are you crazy?" said Sammy. "A lobber is way more powerful than a zapper!"

"I see what you mean," said Sam. "There's no way to know which way the pattern starts without . . . testing it."

Sam took an ominous look up at the nearest wall of RPGs. The squad followed his gaze. Everyone in the squad knew the sound that an RPG made when it was zooming toward your position. It was something nobody ever wanted to hear. And they all thought of just how loud and horrible it would be in an enclosed underground fortress.

"You're pretty tough," Sammy said to Janet. "Do you think you could survive a straight-on RPG hit?"

"Maybe" said Janet. "If I was at full shields, and I had no other injuries, and if I'd gotten like twelve hours of sleep the night before. Then I guess I *maybe* could."

Suddenly, Droopy said: "Hey, I've got an idea about the tiles."

"Oh yeah?" said Mikaleh. "Tell us your idea."

"What if the trick to crossing the tiles," Droopy began, "is to stand on the tile that has a picture of you on it? Because it seems to be working out pretty well for me."

Mikaleh gasped. Everyone looked over. Sure enough, Droopy had wandered out onto the tiled floor. He stood on a tile that had a stylized image of a husk upon it. Droopy looked at the squad and shrugged. All the RPGs stayed where they were.

"That's it!" cried Mikaleh. "It's so simple, we just couldn't think of it. We needed a *really* simple person to show us."

"You're welcome," said Droopy. "I *think*."

"You don't mean that he's right about stepping on a picture of yourself?" Sam asked in shock. "Because if that's the case, the rest of us can't cross."

"No!" said Mikaleh. "It's weight! Droopy weighs almost nothing, right? So I bet that if you put anything slightly heavier than a husk on one of the husk-tiles, it shoots an RPG. And I bet the same is true for the others."

"There's only one way to find out," said Janet, stepping bravely to the edge of the tiles. "I weigh about as much as a chrome husky who has just had seconds at the buffet. Here goes nothing."

Janet dangled a foot onto a tile that featured a crude rendering of a chrome husky. Nothing happened. Janet shifted her full weight upon it. The tile held. The RPGs stayed where they were.

"I think you figured it out, Droopy!" Mikaleh said. "Nice job."

"It was nothing, really," Droopy said.

"This system would actually make a lot of sense," said Sam. "It would go a long way toward filtering out non-husks who didn't know the system, but it would also allow those in the know to pass through quickly. Hmm. Now, I wonder which husk I weigh the same as . . ."

The rest of the squad tried to decide which husk they matched. Mikaleh eventually guessed correctly that she was about pitcher-sized. In this way, the squad carefully crossed the tiled floor, stepping only on tiles with pictures of the husks they had selected. There were several close calls—such as one moment when Janet trailed her foot across a tile decorated with an image of a zapper, and everyone seemed to hear the sound of an RPG trigger beginning to depress—but eventually the entire squad made it to the other side of the tiled floor.

"Whew," said Janet as she hopped off the last chrome husky tile. "That's one of the weirdest crossings I've ever made. And the most stressful."

"For someone who says she's not good at patterns, you did a very good job of not being exploded," said Mikaleh.

"I hope that when we get to your brother, he knows a better way out," Janet said to Droopy. "Because it's too stressful going across that thing."

"Don't worry," said Droopy. "I expect my brother knows another way out of here. At least I hope he does."

The squad inspected the landing on the far side of the tiles where now they stood. There seemed little else to discover, however, and so the adventurers passed through the doorway and into the tunnel beyond.

CHAPTER THIRTEEN

S o I am thinking there will be at least one more," Sam said as they made their way down the darkened corridor.

"One more what?" Sammy whispered.

"One more trap or test," Sam said. "The troll made it sound like there were multiple ones involved. I got the sense that it was a plural kind of a situation."

"Just be ready for anything," Mikaleh told her squad. "Whoever created this place *really* didn't want to make it easy to get to the Last Survivor."

"Yeah?" Janet said sarcastically. "What tipped you off?"

The squad continued down the long corridor, dark except for a few torches in the walls, until they finally spied an open door ahead. It appeared the tunnel led to a well-lit room. At first, it seemed to be filled with husks, or possibly people.

"What are those?" Sammy asked. "Are there humans in that room?"

He reached for his trusty blade.

Mikaleh squinted and looked carefully ahead, but did not pause or adjust her gait. "Not unless they're playing a game where they pretend to stand absolutely still," she said. "Which I don't think they are."

"That doesn't sound like a very fun game, anyway," said Sammy.

"Yeah," agreed Sam. "I would get bored with something like that really fast."

The squad drew close enough to peer into the strange room beyond. It was full of statues. There had to be a hundred of them, Mikaleh reckoned. All had a vaguely humanoid/husk-oid shape, but no defining features. They were all similar, but no two looked completely identical. All of the statues stood on pedestals that were made of concrete and about a foot off the ground. The strangest sight of all, however, was that the statues seemed to be wearing items of clothing. Some wore hats and other had purses slung over their shoulders. Some wore shoes, and others worse vests. One statue was entirely naked except for a chrome fountain pen that had been stuck behind one of its ears.

Mikaleh stepped into the room.

"Be careful," Sam cautioned. "They don't seem to have weapons, but . . . well . . . you never know."

"Ooh," said Janet. "Or maybe it's like the bush disguise."

"Wait," Sam said. "How is this anything like the bush disguise?"

"Well," said Janet, "you put on the bush disguise, and then you waddle over to a bunch of other bushes. And then someone you don't like comes through and just sees a bunch of bushes because they don't look very closely, and then blammo!"

"So this is relevant, how?" said Sam.

Janet rolled her eyes. "For a smart guy, you can be kind of dumb sometimes," she said. "Maybe one of these statues is a real person wearing a disguise. Maybe when we're lulled into a false sense of confidence, they're going to come to life and attack us."

"Oh," said Sam. "That *would* be a good trap, and also a very scary one. I hope that's not the case."

"Remember though . . ." Mikaleh said, taking another cautious step into the room and studying the blank stone faces of the statues. "This isn't designed to take out just anybody who wanders into the room. It's designed to take out visitors who shouldn't be here—like us—who don't know the trick to it."

"So you're saying . . ." said Sammy.

"So I'm saying there's a way we pass through here safely," said Mikaleh. "I'm just not yet sure what it is. And, hey! speaking of passing through safely, look over there."

A few paces inside the room, a path between the statues revealed the opposite wall. Set into it was a door that appeared to be closed and locked. There was also, against the opposite wall, a strange jumble of clothing. There were hats on racks, clothing hanging from hangers, and cases that appeared to be filled with jewelry of all types. It reminded Mikaleh of how the wardrobe room looked if you went backstage at a play—so many costume components laid out for all the actors.

"This just gets weirder and weirder," Sammy said.

Janet had paused to examine one of the statues. This one struck a menacing pose with one hand in the air. Though it had no eyes, it wore a delicate pair of silver-framed glasses. She leaned in close, until she was nearly face to face with it. Closer . . . Closer . . . Closer . . .

"*For goodness sake, don't touch it!*" shouted Sammy.

Janet nearly jumped an inch in her shoes. When she had recovered, she turned around to face Sammy with a stern glower on her face.

"I'm not going to touch it!" she said. "Why would you scare me like that?"

"I didn't mean to," said Sammy. "That was, like, a friendly warning."

Janet turned back to the statue with the glasses.

"I wonder how you would fight one of these things, supposing you had to," Janet said. "I've never attacked something made of rock before. But I can smash rocks to get building material with my pickaxe, so maybe I'd just do that."

"Maybe it would be like fighting a chrome husky," Sammy said. "They're about as tough as stone."

"Flingers are really tough too," Sam added. "I don't know what stuff they're made out of, but it could also be like trying to fight one of them."

"I'm hoping we won't have to fight any of these things," said Mikaleh. She was edging closer to the strange collection of clothing at the far end of the room. Though she walked past many of the statues to get there, none of them moved even in the slightest. Certainly, none came alive and tried to attack her.

Mikaleh arrived at the massive collection of clothing and jewelry beside the far wall. The jewelry was inside glass cases that could be opened.

The lids swung on a hinge. Back in the days before the Storm, when jewelry stores were still a thing, she had seen many collections like this, but never one so large and impressive. She wondered if maybe—when the fighting between the husks and humans ceased and the world became slightly less crazy again—people would have time to think about decorating themselves with fancy sparkly things again. It made her feel sad to think that this probably wouldn't happen for a while. At the same time, it seemed like locating the Last Survivor just might be a way to move the world a step in the right direction.

When she was through inspecting the jewels, she moved over to the door set against the far wall. As the squad watched, she tried it with her hand. Sure enough, it was locked tight.

"Okay," said Mikaleh. "We'll figure this out. Nobody touch anything yet, but take a careful look around. There has to be a trick to it. Something about the clothing and jewelry is connected to the statues. We've just got to figure out what."

The squad joined Mikaleh beside the costumes.

"What can you do with clothing . . ." Sam said, rubbing his chin and thinking hard. "You can put it on and you can take it off. In this way, it's an either/or type of thing. And looking around at these statues, most of them are wearing only one item of jewelry or clothing. Maybe that is also a clue."

"Maybe *we're* supposed to put on the clothing," Janet said brightly. "I think my neck is too big for a lot of those necklaces, but the earrings would fit me. And then the hats. I've always thought that hats were a lot of fun."

"*Us* putting on the clothes?" Sam said doubtfully. "Like we have to be better dressed than the statues? Like it's a contest?"

"I dunno," said Janet with a shrug. "Maybe. Have you got a better idea?"

Sam did not immediately answer.

Sammy looked closely at a heavy wool coat on the clothing rack.

"Maybe I should find a statue that looks cold and give this to it," he said.

"It's possible," said Sam, looking around the room. "But none of them look very cold to me."

"Droopy, you've been awfully silent," said Mikaleh. "Have you got any ideas about what the mystery is here?"

Droopy shrugged. "Ehh," he said. "Husks don't really wear clothes very much. Some people think we're wearing hoodies, but that's really just our skin looking weird. We have pants though, to keep everything PG-13. Even *we* have a sense of modesty."

That made Mikaleh smile.

"Can I try taking one of the items of clothing off a statue?" Janet asked. "What's the worst that could happen?"

"All the statues come alive and attack us," Sam and Sammy said at exactly the same time.

"Yeah," Mikaleh said. "That is probably the worst could happen. But we've got to roll the dice sometimes. Do either of you have a better idea?"

Sam and Sammy looked at each other. It was clear that they did not.

"Okay, then," Mikaleh said to Janet. "I'm inclined to think that we should start testing the water. But do me a favor. Try interacting with some of the clothing on these racks first."

"Ooh, okay!" Janet said. "Maybe I'll look so fancy that the statues will get jealous and tell us how to open the door."

Janet walked to a long rack of clothing. She selected a conical hat like a wizard might wear. It was purple and had blue stars sewn into it.

"I can't resist!" she said. In a single flourish, Janet picked up the wizard's hat and placed it on her head.

Nothing happened.

"C'mon, you statues," Janet said. "You are totally jealous now. Come to life and open the door for us!"

The statues did nothing of the sort, staying quite where they always had been on their pedestals.

"You're all jealous that you're not a wizard," Janet tried. "Pew! Pew! I'm totally casting spells."

The statues remained unmoved.

"Whelp, I don't know what else to tell you," Janet said, turning back to the group. "Those are the only ways I can think of to make a statue jealous."

"Hmm," said Mikaleh. "Maybe we're going about this the wrong way. Instead of putting things on ourselves, we should see if the key is taking things off the statues."

"Just like I'd suggested in the first place," Janet said, removing her wizard hat. "Credit where credit is due."

With that, Janet approached the nearest statue. It wore a brown mink stole around its shoulders like a classic Hollywood actress might have worn to a movie premiere. Janet carefully lifted it off the statue's shoulders. The squad readied themselves for combat and prepared to draw their weapons. When she had completely lifted the stole from the statue's shoulders, Janet jumped back and prepared to draw a weapon of her own.

But as it turned out, no combat would be forthcoming.

The statue did nothing. It did not come to life. And it certainly did not attack them. Neither did any other statue in the room.

"Well, that's no fun," Janet said. "I was hoping we might get to have a little smashy-smashy, blasty-blasty action."

"I wouldn't rule out anything yet," Mikaleh said. "At least now we know the statues don't come to life if you disrobe them. But I'm still so curious. There must be a reason they're here and dressed up like this. It can't just be random. I think we must be missing something. Let's explore some more. Why don't we fan out and look around the rest of the room?"

The squad nodded and began to do exactly that. Each member of the squad set off for a different part of the room, moving between the statues as if in a maze. The squad members searched for anything out of the ordinary, giving each statue they passed a careful inspection, looking for any clue that might enable them to open the door.

Sam was inspecting a statue that was naked except for a bright green Robin Hood hat with a feather, when he saw Droopy a few paces away just leaning against the wall.

"Hey, Droopy!" he called. "That's not cool. This isn't the time to rest. You have to help us. We're all in this together, or have you forgotten?"

"What?" said Droopy. "I haven't forgotten."

Yet to Sam's surprise, he found that Droopy's voice was coming from an entirely different part of the room.

"Wait . . ." said Sam, walking toward Droopy. "Maybe I'm seeing things but—"

And then Sam stood stock still. He realized that he had been addressing one of the statues. One of the statues that looked an awful lot like Droopy, down to the droop in the neck.

"Hey, what gives?" asked actual Droopy, arriving alongside Sam a few moments later. "I'm searching as fast as I can. Why are you criticizing me?"

"I thought you were that statue over there!" Sam said. "Or, I mean, I thought that statue was you. Or . . . Or . . ."

"I get it," said Droopy. "I guess it does look a little like me."

"Hey, everybody," Sam called. "Come over here and take a look at this."

The rest of the squad followed Sam's voice through the maze of statues until they arrived in front of Sam and Droopy. Sam stepped to the side to reveal the statue in question. It was about Droopy's size and shape. Though it had no features, the likeness was unmistakable.

"Wow," said Janet. "That does look like Droopy. At least from across the room."

"And notice something about it," Mikaleh said. "It's not wearing anything. It's the only statue here that's completely naked."

The squad walked around the statue, observing it from all sides. Sure enough, it did not seem to have any article of clothing.

"Aha!" said Sam. "This is making sense now. It's the Last Survivor, and we have to dress him. Well, thank goodness we've got his brother here with us. Droopy, tell us, what would your brother like to wear?"

"Uh, I dunno," said Droopy.

"What?" said Sam. "How can you not know? He's your brother, after all."

"Yeah," said Droopy. "But he was never really into clothes. Most husks aren't. He generally just wore tight little short pants like the rest of us do."

"Seriously?" said Sam. "I have a hard time believing that this trap is related to clothing, and your brother didn't have a favorite outfit."

Droopy shrugged. "Hey, I'd tell you if he did," said Droopy.

"Now that we know about this statue, let's go and have another look at the wall of clothing choices," said Mikaleh. "Droopy, come along too. Maybe something we see there will jog your memory."

"I guess it's possible," Droopy said. He loped after them as the squad returned to the wardrobe arrayed before them.

The members of the squad began to pick through the clothing items and hold them up to Droopy's face. Droopy inspected each one hopefully, as if angling for the hat or shirt or wristwatch to jostle his memory. But nothing seemed to come of it. Time after time, Droopy looked an item over, then shook his head no.

"We could try putting things on the statue at random," Janet suggested. "Maybe when we hit on the correct one, then something good will happen."

"I don't know if I'd want to do that," Mikaleh said. "Mostly, because of all the time it would take. Look at all these clothes. We'd be here for weeks. And I don't think we have enough food or water to last that long. There's got to be something else."

"Maybe there is some clue we're not seeing," said Sam. "There could be some pattern that will show us the way."

"Do you mean like a fabric pattern?" asked Sammy. "Because there are a lot of them."

"It could be something to do with fabric," Sam said.

Mikaleh walked a few paces away from the racks of clothes. She found that when she needed to think, it sometimes helped to walk around. Once she was a few paces away, Mikaleh chanced to look back at her colleagues digging through the racks of clothes.

That was when it struck her.

"Hey," she said. "These clothes are all similar colors. Looking at them all in one big group like this, you can see it."

"Really?" said Sammy. "I see plenty of different colors. Like, this hat is blue. This shirt is white. These shoes are green."

"Yes," Mikaleh said. "But notice which colors you *don't* see."

To make her point, she reached into her inventory and brought out the golden key with the red handle.

"She's right," Janet said. "Nothing here is gold or red. Even the jewelry is all sterling silver. Huh. I never noticed it before."

"And we know that this key is associated with the Last Survivor," said Mikaleh. "I've got the crazy idea that there might just be *one* thing here that's red and gold. And if we can find it, we might be able to solve this puzzle. Start digging through the clothes again, but this time, you're only looking for red and for gold!"

The squad began their inventory anew. Things moved much more quickly now because they knew what they were looking for. Before long, Sammy emerged from the rack of clothing with an item held high.

"Found it!" he cried.

Everyone looked. Sammy was holding a pair of short pants, just like Droopy wore. The only difference was that these were bright red with gold stitching on the seams.

"If there's anything else around here that's red and gold, I didn't see it," Sammy said.

"How're we gonna get it on the statue?" Janet asked.

"It looks like it has Velcro in the back," Sammy said, flipping the pair of shorts over.

Sure enough, it did.

With Sammy leading the way, the group hustled over to where the statue of the Last Survivor waited near the wall. As everyone else looked on, Sammy helped the statue into its shorts, and Velcroed them up in the back.

"There you go, champ," Sammy said like he was putting clothes on a baby. "You're a big boy now."

No sooner were these words out of his mouth than the statue that looked so much like Droopy began to rotate on its base.

"Ahh!" said Sammy. "I was just kidding! You've always been a big boy!"

The statue rotated until it faced the far wall where the door out of the room stood closed and locked. As the squad watched, the door opened by itself.

"Wow!" said Janet. "It actually worked."

"Yes," said Mikaleh. "I had a feeling that it would."

"I hope we're close to finding the Last Survivor," said Janet as they walked toward the open doorway. "How much bigger can this place be?"

"It's already proven itself to be much larger than it looked," said Mikaleh. "But I have a feeling we must be getting close."

And with that, the squad passed through the doorway and into the hallway beyond.

CHAPTER FOURTEEN

They headed down a torch-lined hallway that looked similar to the ones they had passed before. Very abruptly, Droopy stopped walking. It was as though whatever force powered him had suddenly run out of juice.

The rest of the squad stopped too.

"Droopy, what's wrong?" Mikaleh asked.

"My brother . . ." he said. "I can smell him. He's very close. I think we have nearly arrived at wherever he is being kept."

They had.

When Droopy began moving again, they traveled just a few more yards down the hall and discovered a tall metal door. It did not appear to be locked. Mikaleh took a deep breath, looked at her squad, and cracked it open. Beyond was a very strange room. It was wide and had a very high ceiling. In the center of the room was a ring of lava, like a moat. In the center of the ring was a large crate, like a shipping container. The container had a door set into the front of it, and the door had a keyhole. Even from across the room,

Mikaleh could see that the outline of the keyhole was edged in red and gold. A small bridge led over the moat of lava. To either side of the moat stood two very large blasters. They stood on top of big X's that had been drawn on the floor. They were absolutely immense, and their glowing eyes seemed to radiate danger.

As Mikaleh looked over the situation, the rest of the squad joined her.

"That's got to be where the Last Survivor is kept," said Janet excitedly. "We've finally found him."

"I think you're right," Mikaleh said.

"A couple of blasters, huh?" Sammy observed. "They don't look so tough. I mean, yes they do look tough. But not tougher than us. That's what I meant to say."

"Okay," Mikaleh said. "I'll lead the way, but everyone be careful. Whoever designed this fortress clearly was fond of putting tricks and puzzles in the rooms. I can see no reason why this final room would be any different."

Mikaleh pushed the door fully open, and they stepped into the strange large room.

The blasters immediately stood at attention. They looked around at their new guests. Then their eyes squinted angrily.

"Okay, gentlemen," Mikaleh said loudly. "I'm going to give you one chance—and one chance only—to cooperate. As you can see, my squad and I are armed to the teeth. And, boy oh boy, do we ever know how to use these weapons. This being the case, I really think you ought to—"

"The Last Survivor!" one of the blasters cried. "Why is he with you?"

Both blasters stared wide-eyed at Droopy as he hunched at the back of the group.

"This makes no sense," said the other blaster. "How can he be out here, when we know he's in there?"

Mikaleh immediately realized that the blasters had made the same mistake as the troll who had guarded the first door. Her mind raced as she searched for a way to use this to their advantage.

"Waaaait," said the first blaster. "How do we know that's really him?"

The second blaster did not immediately respond.

"Is he talking to me?" Mikaleh asked Droopy.

"Could be," Droopy said. "But blasters also have very little in the way of internal monologue."

"What does that mean?" Janet asked.

"It means they *say* things instead of *thinking* things," Droopy told her.

"Oh, you mean talking to themselves," Janet said. "That's not so weird. I do that all the time!"

Mikaleh stepped forward. "Look, I think both of you need to just go away, clock out, do whatever you do when you go off duty, and get out of here," she said.

"This still makes no sense," said the second blaster. "And when I get confused, it just makes me want to blast something."

"Yes," said the first blaster. "My motto is always blast things first and ask questions later."

"Agreed," said the second one. "There's no way we're going to get in trouble if we just blast these guys. We're blasters. They gave us this job because we do exactly that."

"Wait," said Mikaleh. "You guys don't want to do that."

"Why?" said both blasters together.

"The moment you guys start shooting, then we'll start shooting," said Mikaleh. "And we're going to win that battle."

"Yes, but then you lose the war," said the blaster. "I mean . . . I'm not trying to be dramatic. It will be a very small war, just confined to this room, but you will lose it."

"How?" said Mikaleh.

"Don't you know what these things are that we're standing on?" said the first blaster.

"X's drawn in chalk," Mikaleh answered.

"Right," said the blaster. "But *underneath* them are pressure plates. And if either one of us is not standing on our pressure plate, then that little cell with the Last Survivor inside of it gets lowered into the lava forever. It's all automatic."

Droopy put his hand to his mouth.

"Will it kill him?" Mikaleh said, as much to Droopy as to the blasters.

"Nobody knows," said one of the blasters. "But he'll be trapped down there in the lava forever. Nobody will be able to get him out. As for me, I would probably die of boredom. It's boring enough in his cell, but at least he has things to read and do in there. But if your whole existence was just sitting around waiting for lava to cool? Omigosh. Snooze Central."

"And there are other layers to this kind of security," the other blaster said proudly. "For example, you can only get in to rescue the Last Survivor if you have the key, right? But the key's presence makes him weak. So then he's not dangerous to us, but then also, the lava kills him right away if the key is near."

"Oh, no question," said the first blaster. "Right away."

"But look," said the second blaster. "Why are you confusing us like this? Why does it look like you've got the Last Survivor out there? He shouldn't be out. And if he is out, he should almost definitely be blasted. I'm not sure who you are, or how you got past the troll and all the other tests, but I know that something is very wrong here."

"Again, I feel like blasting is the answer," said the first blaster. "You can just never go wrong when you decide to blast things."

"And it's fun," said the second blaster.

"Oh, yes," said the first. "So much fun."

The blasters' eyes glowed as if they were considering unleashing their laser weapons upon the squad. Mikaleh's stomach sank. Whoever had designed this place seemed to have kept one step ahead of them. The traps in the other rooms had worked, and there was no reason she could see to think that these blasters were bluffing (not least because they did not seem smart enough to).

To Mikaleh, the only option seemed to be to run back the way they had come, and to shield themselves from the blasters' lasers on the other side of the door. Perhaps then she would be able to think of some way around this conundrum.

Yet before she could move, Mikaleh felt someone brush past her. It was Droopy! He bravely strode to the front of the squad.

"Droopy, what are you doing?" said Sam.

"Yeah," Sammy added. "Quick, get back behind us. We've got shields and lots of health. You're a wispy little husk. One big blast from those guys and you're smithereens. I don't know if you know what smithereens is, but trust me, you don't want to be it."

"No," said Droopy, staying right where he was. "Trust me. I may not be tougher than a blaster, but I'm definitely smarter than these two."

Then Droopy looked up at the blasters.

"So you guys are worried about getting in trouble, eh?" he said.

"Well, of course," said the first blaster, continuing to charge. "A blaster's prime directives are to blast things and avoid being blamed for stuff. Anybody who knows blasters would know that."

"Then I'll tell you the truth," Droopy said. "I'm the brother of the Last Survivor."

Mikaleh had never heard a blaster gasp before. It was a strange sound, like all the air being sucked out of a room. The blasters seemed unsure if they should continue charging.

"The Last Survivor doesn't have a brother," said the first blaster, though it was clear his heart was not in it.

"And how do you know that?" asked Droopy.

"Because . . . Because . . . Because   everybody knows that he doesn't have a brother," the blaster insisted.

"Sometimes everybody can be wrong," said Droopy. "Why do you think I look *exactly* like him? It's not a coincidence. It would be weird if I looked this much like him and he *wasn't* my brother."

"He's got you there," said the second blaster with a grin.

"Shut up," said the first.

"I'm going to tell you how you can not get in trouble and also live to blast another day," said

Droopy. "You're going to get out of the way and let me open that cell and free my brother. If you do that, me and my friends might agree to let you survive. How do you think we've gotten this far? Do you think it's an accident that we're here?"

Mikaleh had never seen Droopy so focused and aggressive. It made her feel sort of proud.

"These are the best humans in any squad," Droopy continued. "They've proven just how brave humans can be. And how tough. And how clever."

"But that's blasphemy!" the first blaster said. "Humans are always the enemy."

"Maybe that's the official consensus," said Droopy. "But these humans have been very dedicated and very helpful to me. Ask yourself if there's any way they could have gotten this far if I'm not telling you the truth."

"Gee," said one of the blasters. "I guess they do look pretty tough."

"And smart," said the other blaster. "Those two that look alike even have glasses."

"But if you agree to drop all this nonsense now, and let us pass through and free my brother," Droopy continued, "I promise that you will be allowed to go peacefully. And you won't be in any kind of trouble. Bygones will be bygones, and so forth."

It was clear from the expressions that came to the blasters' faces that this was a pleasant idea.

"But if you don't . . ." Droopy said menacingly, "then I can't promise exactly what will happen to you, but this squad is eventually going to free my brother one way or another. And when he gets loose, I'll tell him what you did. And then you're going to be in the worst trouble of all."

The blasters clearly did not like the way this sounded. They looked at each other. Then—to the great relief of Droopy and the squad—they stopped charging their lasers.

"You *promise* we won't be in trouble?" asked the first. "Not even a little bit? Because sometimes being just a little bit in trouble is unpleasant too. It's like having someone who says they're not mad at you all day, when really you can tell that they are."

"Ooh, I hate it when people do that," said the second blaster.

"No," said Droopy. "You won't be in any kind of trouble. Just stay where you are. Keep standing on your pressure plates."

"Okay," said the first blaster. "We can do that."

"Yeah," said the second. "That's what we usually do all the time anyway."

Droopy looked back at Mikaleh and smiled.

Mikaleh patted Droopy on his bony back, and they began to cross the bridge that led over the pit of lava to the cell beyond.

"I cannot believe that worked," Mikaleh said. "Nice going."

"Thank you," Droopy said. "I decided a direct approach was probably the best one. Now let's hurry up and get my brother out of there before they change their minds."

"Okay," said Mikaleh. "But there's something I have to remind you of, Droopy. Your brother is immensely powerful, and he was locked up because he was dangerous. I'm not sure what he's going to be like, but I can't allow someone who is bent on destroying everybody to be set loose upon the world again. You know that—right?"

"Yes," Droopy said with a sad nod. "I wouldn't want him to do that either."

They crossed the bridge and soon stood before the strange cell where the Last Survivor was imprisoned. Mikaleh drew the key from her inventory. The red crystal blaster eye in the handle sparkled in the glow of the lava moat, and the gold gleamed. Mikaleh put the key into the lock and turned . . .

CHAPTER FIFTEEN

I t was like looking in a mirror.

Well, for Droopy that's what it must be like, thought Mikaleh.

For the rest of the squad it was like seeing two Droopys standing right in front of each other.

As Droopy stared into the cell, the Last Survivor stared back out at him. He looked just like Droopy, down to the strange crook in his neck and his tight blue short pants.

"Brother?" the Last Survivor said. "Is that really you? I can't believe . . . Look out, bro! Humans! I'll save us with my . . . with my . . ."

The Last Survivor made several dramatic gestures with his arms, as though he expected powerful energy beams to shoot. Instead nothing happened. The Last Survivor noticed this and eventually stopped waving his arms.

"Oh, right," he said. "The key."

His face fell, and he hung his head.

"I'm the famous Last Survivor, and I can't even protect my own brother. I can't do anything right."

"First of all, there's no reason for you to protect me . . . at least not from them," said Droopy. "They're humans, but they're nice. They helped me to come here and rescue you. I couldn't have done this without them!"

"Friendly humans?" said the Last Survivor. "I guess that might be *technically* possible . . ."

"It's more than technically possible," said Droopy. "It's real. They're nice and you can trust them."

The Last Survivor considered this for a moment.

"Very well," he said. "If you, my own brother, say they are trustworthy, then I will assume that they are."

"So, obviously, if we got you out of that nasty old cell, then it means we've got the gold key with the red handle," Droopy pointed out. "Tell us what you want us to do, brother. We could throw it into some of this lava and melt it forever."

Mikaleh stepped forward and cleared her throat.

"Not to be a buzzkill, Droopy," she said. "But you'll remember what we discussed when my squad first agreed to come along on this journey. Your brother seems like a good guy, but I will need to be convinced that he won't use his powers for evil before I agree to get rid of the one thing that can control him."

"But . . ." Droopy said, his lower lip beginning to tremble from emotion. (And because his lips were old and rotting—as the lips of all husks are—Mikaleh was a bit worried that it might tremble right off.) "You seem like a nice person, Mikaleh. Why can't you just be nice about this too? Why can't you just throw the key into the lava so nobody can ever do something like this to my brother again?"

The Last Survivor spoke up.

"Brother—or Droopy, as I see you are now called—I think your human friend is right. I have had years in my cell to think about these things and to figure out the next step. You should certainly *not* destroy the key, for it is still very much needed. And your quest, I'm afraid, is not yet over."

"What?" Droopy said.

"If you have come this far, then you know very much," the Last Survivor said. "You know more than most humans or husks have ever guessed. But you do not quite know everything. Now it is time for me to tell you the rest of the story."

"What're you talking about?" said Droopy.

"It is true that when our worlds came together—the husk world within the Storm and the human world beyond it—I was in the wrong place at the wrong time, and was blessed—or cursed—with remarkable powers. But I was not the only one."

"Right," said Droopy. "There was also the blaster who got crystallized or something? And his eye is now the ruby in the key."

"Yes," agreed the Last Survivor. "But he was incidental. There was another who survived it but was, like me, blessed with awesome powers."

"Another Last Survivor?" said Droopy.

"So really, you're not the Last Survivor," said Mikaleh. "You're the Last-but-one Survivor."

The Last Survivor nodded.

"There was a taker who was standing right next to me when the joining of worlds happened. We were both affected in the same way. I looked at him and he looked at me, and we both knew we had been infected with the same abilities. So I used my powers—too aggressively, I now understand. I used them to fight humans, and to fight other husks, and really just anybody who was annoying me at the moment. But this taker kept his powers secret. He didn't tell anybody what he could do. He used his powers only in secret, and to eliminate his enemies. In doing so, he rose gradually in the power structure of the husks and mist monsters."

"Waaaaaaait," said Droopy. "Is this guy going to be—"

"The Grand Taker," said the Last Survivor. "Yes. That's him indeed."

"Who is the Grand Taker?" Mikaleh asked.

"One of the most important creatures from our side of the Storm," Droopy said. "Like humans, we're not organized enough right now to have a government, but everybody can kind of figure out who is the most powerful. Like how your squad, Mikaleh, is known as the most powerful among the surviving humans. The Grand Taker is known as most powerful among the husks and mist monsters."

"Yes," agreed the Last Survivor. "My brother is right. But where your squad probably rose to fame and power through practicing and getting really good at defending your forts and shield generators—"

"There's no 'probably' about it," interjected Janet.

The Last Survivor smiled.

"The Grand Taker got to where he is by using these same powers I have in a secret, deceptive way. When I was captured and imprisoned here,

I realized quickly what had happened. It was the Grand Taker. He had convinced the others that I was too dangerous, and that I could not be allowed to roam free. But what he was really doing was consolidating his power. He knew that I was the only one who could ever hope to match him. By convincing others to shutter me away, he knew that he could rule unchallenged."

"That's lousy," said Droopy. "I had no idea that had happened."

"As I've said, I had many years here to think about how to solve this problem if I was ever freed," said the Last Survivor. "And I think the only way I can set things right again and prevent the Grand Taker from hurting anybody else . . . is to take the thing that rendered me powerless— the gold and ruby key—to him. Only when his powers are contained, like mine are now, will there be any chance of defeating him."

"We can totally help you do that, bro!" Droopy said, enthusiasm returning to him. "And it won't just be a husk versus a taker. We've got the most butt-kicking human squad with us too."

The Last Survivor smiled thoughtfully.

"Yes," he said. "But the Grand Taker is liable to have his own helpers and assistants. It will probably take all that we have got to defeat him. The good news is that he is not far from here. In another part of Twine Peaks quite close by there is a very tall mountain. The Grand Taker lives at the top. If we go there straightaway, we can reach him before he learns that I have been released. He will not be prepared. That gives us our best chance of achieving a swift and decisive victory. Tell me, did you alert anyone that you were breaking me out?"

"No," said Droopy. "The 'sploders outside thought that I was you, and you were being returned to prison. The troll also thought the same thing. And these two blasters don't exactly know what to think."

"Yeah, those two aren't very bright," said the Last Survivor. "I've had lots of time to watch them through the bars on my cell. In that case, it sounds like we are very well positioned to act decisively. And I know another secret that will also help us. On the far side of this room is a secret exit. I have seen the creatures guarding me use it to come in and out. We can use it to get topside again without anybody knowing."

"Well, this sounds really good," said Droopy. "What are we waiting for?"

"Hang on just one more moment," said Mikaleh. "I have to have a word with my squad."

Mikaleh motioned for Sam, Sammy, and Janet to join her.

"Look," she said to them. "This journey has gotten much longer and much stranger than I ever thought it would, way back when some pitchers threw messages at us. I just want all of you to know that you don't have to go any farther if you don't want to. I thought reaching the Last Survivor would be the end of it, but it looks like there's a bit more to go. I wouldn't blame any of you if you didn't feel like you could continue at this point. We've faced some challenges and risks getting this far, but if the Last Survivor is telling us the truth, then I think this Grand Taker might present the biggest challenge of all."

Mikaleh genuinely did not know how her squad might react. They were all exhausted, she imagined, and all had the unsatisfying feeling of having been told that the end they'd thought was in sight was really not the end at all.

"Of *course* we're with you!" Janet boomed. "At least, I know that I am. You couldn't get rid of me if you tried!"

"And I'm not going anywhere . . . I'm just learning too much!" exclaimed Sam. "Forget writing the book on husks. By the time all of this is over, I'll be the author of several volumes."

"And you can't really separate me from Sam," said Sammy. "So I'm in this too. I want to see how this ends."

"Okay then," Mikaleh said. "If you're all agreed, I'll go and tell Droopy and the Last Survivor. But get ready for a test like we've never faced before. I think it's only going to get crazier from here."

CHAPTER SIXTEEN

They climbed up a long winding tunnel that took them away from the chamber in which the Last Survivor had been imprisoned for lo these many years. (The blasters had been too afraid to turn around, much less to abandon the pressure plates on which they stood.) The Last Survivor had been correct. Though the journey to the top was long and arduous, they soon saw daylight above them in the tunnel.

"I just hope that this spits us out somewhere I can harvest wood, stone, or metal," said Janet. "I still feel naked with nothing to build with. And we're going to be trapped if we can't find a way to cross that lava."

Janet need not have worried. The tunnel opened on to a desolate plain, far from the fortress and the island of lava. There were several stunted, sickly trees dotting the landscape. Janet made short work of them with her pickaxe, harvesting them hastily.

"At least now my wood reserves are full," she said. "I'd like to have stone and metal too, but beggars can't be choosers, I suppose."

In the distance, a mountain of black ore rose into the clouds.

"There is our destination," said the Last Survivor.

They hurried toward it.

"I'm impressed that you can move so quickly," Mikaleh said to the Last Survivor. "You just got out of a cell."

"You should see me when I haven't been in a cell," the Last Survivor said. "I'm the fastest husk around!"

They ran across the forbidding black landscape, and the mountain ahead of them slowly grew larger. At one point, Mikaleh risked a glance back over her shoulder. As she was afraid she might, she saw several small creatures in the far distance, heading after them.

"What is it?" asked Janet.

"'Sploders," Mikaleh said. "I was afraid this might happen. Somehow, they've found out what we did. They're racing to reach the mountain before we do, so they can inform the Grand Taker."

"Yes," said Janet thoughtfully. "Or maybe they're just coming to throw explosives at us because that's what they like to do."

"Either way, we have to keep going as fast as we can," Mikaleh said.

After what seemed like an eternity of running, they reached the foot of the mountain.

"I know how we can put some more distance between ourselves and the 'sploders," Mikaleh said. "Instead of taking the winding paths up to the top, Janet can build us a ramp that will be almost vertical. We can run straight up it. Then, when we get to the top, we can destroy it so the 'sploders can't use it."

"Sounds good to me," Janet said. "Everybody get out of the way!"

Janet began to build like she had never built before. Compared to this feat, the bridge across the lava lake had only been an amateur's audition. This was a true test of everything that Janet could do. The boards seemed to spring from her hands as if by magic and to assemble themselves into a bridge. The squad raced up after her. Higher and higher, they climbed. Yet the 'sploders still pursued them.

"Come on," cried Mikaleh. "We're almost to the top. Keep it up Janet!"

Janet did. Faster than seemed possible, the squad had climbed up the side of the mountain, and so had Droopy and the Last Survivor. As they scuttled onto the mountain and off Janet's bridge, Mikaleh cried: "Okay, guys. Let 'em have it!"

Down at the foot of the mountain, the 'sploders had reached the base of the ramp and were beginning to use it. The squad drew their weapons and unloaded with everything they had. The mountain seemed to shake with the thunder of guns—and a few grenades for good measure. In a matter of seconds, the ramp was totally destroyed, and the 'sploders found themselves falling back to earth. It would take them a long time to climb the mountain on their own. For now, they were out of the picture.

The top of the mountain was not perfectly pointed, but instead a strange rocky plateau.

"Yes, this is where he lives," said the Last Survivor. "We have come to the right place. Now we have only to summon and defeat the Grand Taker."

"Okay," said Mikaleh. "How do we do that?"

"Probably by yelling for him," said the Last Survivor. "Yelling is good for getting most people's attention. I don't see why this situation would be any different."

The Last Survivor cleared his throat and cupped his hands to his mouth.

"All right, Grand Taker!" he shouted. "I know what you are! Come out and face me!"

After a moment, another voice boomed.

"WHO DARES TO TALK TO ME LIKE THAT?"

Mikaleh looked around for a source. Then, from out of the clouds above the mountaintop, a group of takers descended. There were perhaps ten of them. But there was no question as to which one might be the Grand Taker. He was a good three feet taller than the rest, and his orange eyes glowed brighter than the others. While the rest of the takers landed on the mountaintop, the Grand Taker remained hovering in the sky.

"It's me!" the Last Survivor shouted.

"You?" the Grand Taker said. "What makes you think I should know who you are, little husk? Why are you up on my mountaintop?"

"Have you really already forgotten?" said the Last Survivor.

Droopy stepped next to his brother. The Grand Taker's face finally showed recognition. A mix of emotions seemed to cascade over him. The overriding one, however, was horror.

"It can't be!" the Grand Taker cried. "How did you get out? And your stupid twin brother is here too?"

"Hey!" Sam and Sammy said in unison.

Then Sam added: "Don't pick on twins."

"You did a horrible thing when you imprisoned me like that," said the Last Survivor.

"Oh yeah," said the Grand Taker. "That's just your opinion. And I don't want to hear anything more from you. You're about to really regret coming here."

The Grand Taker extended his hands aggressively, as if casting spells. But they seemed to be the kind of spells that didn't do anything, because nothing happened.

"What in the world?" the Grand Taker said. "My powers . . . the key! You've brought it here with you. Well then, you are as vulnerable as I am. And in that case, my friends will make short work of you. At them, lads!"

The group of takers flung themselves forward. Mikaleh and her squad bravely stepped in front of Droopy and the Last Survivor.

"Okay, guys," she said. "You know what to do."

They did.

Mikaleh took out her legendary assault rifle and laid down a line of fire that had the takers leaping for cover in all directions. Janet produced her sledgehammer and began smacking the scattering takers on their heads. It made a satisfying knocking sound each time she connected. Sam took out a shotgun and put down any of the takers who ducked out of the way of Janet's swings. And Sammy drew his sword and charged forward, then leapt in the air and somersaulted over the takers. Then, as always, he began attacking them from behind.

After just a few moments, there were no takers left standing.

The Grand Taker still floated above. His expression showed sheer astonishment.

"What just happened?" he cried, bewildered.

Droopy spoke up.

"I've brought along the best, most capable human squad there is! If you couldn't tell before, you're really in trouble!"

The Grand Taker began to consider his options. His eyes darted this way and that.

"He's getting ready to run," said the Last Survivor. "Mikaleh, don't let him get away. Right now, he and I both have our powers restrained by the presence of the key. If he gets too far away, his powers will come back. As long as you stay close to the key, your squad will be safe from him. But I can't say the same for anybody else. We need to catch him and end this now."

"Say no more!" said Mikaleh.

She let her rifle fall from her hands and sprinted straight at the Grand Taker. The floating creature turned and tried to fly away, but it was too late. Mikaleh leapt through the air and landed on its back with a thud. Then she gripped one of the Grand Taker's arms and began to twist it back . . . farther . . . farther . . . farther . . .

"Ow!" the Grand Taker cried. "Stop doing that."

Mikaleh did no such thing.

"Ow!" it cried. "I'm used to having magical powers. *This is so much harder without magical powers!*"

Eventually, the Grand Taker stopped struggling as much. As it lessened its objections, it slowly drifted back down to the surface of the mountaintop.

Janet ran forward and swept its legs out from under it with a single swing of her sledgehammer.

"Ack!" the Grand Taker cried.

It fell face forward. Now Mikaleh sat on its back like a police officer making an arrest. When the Grand Taker finally stopped squirming, the rest of the squad drew near.

"That was amazing!" said Sam, quite astounded.

"Yeah," added Sammy. "That was nice jumping, for a non-ninja."

Mikaleh looked up at the Last Survivor.

"Do you want me to finish him off?" she asked.

Suddenly, the Last Survivor's face fell. (Given that he was essentially a zombie, and rotting away, this was nearly literal.) The Last Survivor looked very grim, but also very resolute. Mikaleh did not know what to make of it.

The Last Survivor turned to face his brother.

"Droopy, as you are now called, I have something very challenging to tell you," he said. "During my time of confinement, I struggled with how the Grand Taker could ever be defeated. It presents something of a strange conundrum. Both of us have been given too much power. In order for the world to be safe, both of us would always have to be kept in proximity to the key. I don't think that will be possible. You've just proven how, by assembling a determined crew, you were able to break me out of a fortress that was full of powerful traps. If we put the Grand Taker in a similar fortress, eventually his own followers would doubtless find a way to break *him* out as well. I'm afraid we need to find a more permanent solution."

"I don't like the sound of this," Droopy said.

The Last Survivor walked over to where Mikaleh had the Grand Taker pinned with his arm behind his back.

When the Last Survivor was but a few paces away, the Grand Taker began to shout: "No! No! Stay away! Please, don't let him do it!"

"I don't understand what is happening," Droopy said. "Do what?"

"The Grand Taker is squirming like this because he has felt what I have also felt," said the Last Survivor. "Namely, we are both charged with a terrible power. But we are oppositely charged, like magnets."

The Last Survivor leaned forward, very close to the Grand Taker. The Grand Taker squirmed and cowered.

"He can sense it too," the Last Survivor pronounced.

"I don't understand," said Droopy.

"If he and I were to touch one another, the polarizing powers within us would form another conjunction between worlds," the Last Survivor said. "I am not completely sure how it would work, but I have the sense that we would be transported to where we used to be. To the place where the rest of our world still is. One thing that's for certain is we wouldn't be here anymore."

"So you're saying . . ." Droopy began.

"I'm afraid so," said the Last Survivor.

"But you can't leave now!" Droopy howled. "I went to all this trouble to find you. I've been missing you for all of these years. And now you just want to leave. Poof! Just like that?"

"I'm sorry," the Last Survivor said to his brother. "But I think it's the only way we can make the world safe again."

"You can't be serious," said Droopy.

"I'm sorry, but I am," said the Last Survivor.

"No!" said Droopy. "I refuse to let you do this. There has to be another way!"

Suddenly, the Grand Taker's sheer terror and fear seemed to let him push through the pain of having his arm pinned. He twisted and bucked unexpectedly, and threw Mikaleh off his back.

The squad circled around him as though he were an escaped animal they were attempting to catch. The Last Survivor began to approach, but the Grand Taker moved away each time. Takers were known for their evasive action, and their ability to fly and seemingly disappear and reappear at will. Now that the Grand Taker was loose again, the prospect of recapturing him was far from certain.

"No," the Grand Taker cried. "You'll never catch me and take me away with you. I like being here and being so powerful. I won't give it up!"

Then began the craziest chase that any of the squad had ever experienced. They chased the Grand Taker all over the mountaintop, trying to corral him. The squad seemed unable to catch the ethereal beast, but neither was it able to escape. Whenever there seemed to be an opening, in the circle they made around it, someone was able to herd the taker back to the center.

Then the Grand Taker made an abrupt fake in one direction, and then headed in the other. Sam and Sammy sprang out to block him, but they sprang too hard and ended up running into each other. Both of them went tumbling to the ground. While they were disoriented, the Grand Taker saw an opening where he could sprint past them and jump down the mountainside, evading capture.

The Grand Taker smiled an evil smile. He juked past the prone Sam and Sammy and headed to the edge of the mountain. As he neared the edge, he took a moment to look back at the Last Survivor and gloat.

"This was the best you could do, eh?" he said. "The next time I see you, you'll be back in a prison again. So long!"

And as the Grand Taker began to make his final leap off the side of the mountain, his foot caught on something and instead he fell back to the ground.

Mikaleh realized that what he'd tripped on was nothing other than Droopy's foot. Droopy had, at the last moment, stuck out a leg to stop him. And it had worked.

Mikaleh once more pounced on the Grand Taker, and this time Janet also sat on him for good measure. Still, the full efforts of the two women combined were barely enough to hold him down.

"Hurry," Mikaleh said. "He's going to get loose again. If there's something you need to do, you'd better do it!"

The Last Survivor looked at his brother.

"Droopy . . ." he said, nearly dumbfounded. "Why did you help us?"

Droopy shrugged.

"You're my brother," he said. "I'd do anything for you. Even if it means I'll be sad because you're leaving."

The Last Survivor opened his arms and gave his brother a hug. (Mikaleh had never seen husks do this before. Of all the strange sights she had encountered since this adventure had begun, this might have been the strangest.) Then the Last Survivor turned to the Grand Taker. He reached down and grabbed the Grand Taker by his bony hand.

For an instant nothing happened. Then there was a sound, or perhaps, a strange absence of sound, like all the noise had been sucked out of the universe. There was nothing to smell or taste. A strange nothingness pervaded. Then there was a tremendously bright white flash. And a sound so loud it sounded like nothing at all.

EPILOGUE

Mikaleh opened her eyes and saw that she was on her back, looking up at the sky. It was a nasty, cloudy Twine Peaks sky, but still the sky. She sat up and realized that she was in a field at the base of the mountain. She looked at the top of the mountain and saw that it had been disfigured somehow, as if by an explosion. Mikaleh realized she had been blown all the way down the mountainside.

She stood up and looked around. On the ground nearby were Sam and Sammy, both still opening their eyes and trying to figure out what had happened. Janet, who was already upright, bounded over to help them up.

Mikaleh walked over too. "Are you guys all right?" Mikaleh asked.

"I think so," said Sammy, rising to his feet. "What on earth was that?"

"We got blown down the mountain," said Sam. "The force of the Last Survivor and Grand Taker being sucked into another world must have created a rip in space-time like an explosion. Whew. We're lucky to be alive."

Janet looked around.

"Is that it then?" she said. "Is it finally over? But with all of that effort . . . what did we actually do?"

"We solved a mystery, and we made sure that a very dangerous weapon isn't in this world anymore," Mikaleh said. "Two weapons, really. I'd call that pretty good for a couple days of work."

"I guess so," said Janet. "If you put it in those terms, we did a heck of a lot. All right! I like it!"

"Has, uh, has anybody seen Droopy?" Mikaleh asked.

The squad looked around their immediate vicinity.

"He's very lightweight, so the explosion probably blew him far away," Sam said.

Now the squad looked toward the distant horizon. And there, they saw a skinny husk with a crooked neck righting itself.

The squad bounded over.

"Are you okay?" Mikaleh asked.

Droopy brushed himself off.

"Yes, I'm okay . . . I think. Maybe my neck is a little extra droopy now. But what're you gonna do."

"Droopy, I can't believe you did that," said Mikaleh. "That Grand Taker would have escaped if it hadn't been for you."

"I guess," Droopy said.

The husk looked sad.

"I just feel bad that I didn't get to spend more time with my brother," Droopy said. "We went through all of that to find him. And then—poof!— it was over."

"I know," said Mikaleh. "And that's why I'm so proud of you. You did the right thing even though you knew it would bring a result that was painful for you. Not everybody would have done something like that."

"Yes," said Janet. "And wherever your brother is now, I'm sure he's in a better place."

"I think that is actually, literally true," Sam added. "They went back to the husk dimension within the Storm. Life will be much more suited to him there."

"I guess," Droopy said. "I wonder if I'll ever see him again."

"You never can tell about these things," Mikaleh said. "But when the world has gone crazy, and husks and humans are fighting each other, and universes are crashing into one another . . . well, who's to say what's unlikely. Certainly not me."

"Well now," said Droopy. "That is a comforting thought."

Droopy gazed at the horizon for a moment, and then looked back at the squad.

"Speaking of husks and humans fighting, I don't think I would want to fight you guys after all we've been through," he said. "I realize that our journey is over, and I should probably get back to my husk friends. But I don't feel quite so aggressive now. If you ever see me in the course of a husk raid on some humans, please know that my heart's not in it. And if I ever happen to smack and bite your shield a few times before I realize it's you, please don't take it personally."

"No worries," Mikaleh said with a laugh. "And we'll all make a point to try to aim high if we see a husk who has a particularly crooked neck coming our way."